THE EXORCISM OF MILLER'S CROSSING

Miller's Crossing Book Four

David Clark

CONTENTS

1

Days turned into a week in Miller's Crossing, but only the calendar recorded the passage of time. The sun continued to come up in the morning and disappear in the evening, but not even the light of day could crack through the darkness that loomed over the town. This wasn't the darkness of night or a storm cloud, this darkness was heavy and wet. Like the type you find in the furthest and deepest corner of a leaky basement, down where mold, mildew, and the fear of things that *go boo* lived. The difference here, the things that *go boo* were walking the streets.

Its citizens had taken refuge at the high school or their own homes since what they called "the event." Most only braved a daylight raid for supplies, but even that was a tentative and dangerous effort. No one moved alone or blindly. They always checked around the corner to make sure nothing was there before going further. Only a few stores remained open. Two days after the event, Ted Barton moved into the back storeroom of his local grocery and mercantile. Every morning he stepped outside and looked to see what was around and then re-locked the door; that was the only time he actually went outside. The rest of the time he stayed in the store, watching and waiting for anyone who may come in need of food or supplies. When the sun started to dip and shadows stretched across the street and his storefront, he retreated to the safety of his back storeroom. The sound from the portable television Ted had kept back there since the Cuban Missile Crisis battled against the screaming and howling outside.

Two days after the event, Lewis Tillingsly closed down the roads into and out of town under the guise of roadwork. He even went as far as sending a press release to all the neighboring towns to be read on the radio, and to the Lynchburg local news. To further sell the story, he and Frank Michaels took two farm tractors out and dug up large sections of the road, leaving piles of dirt as obstructions. To an outsider, it would look like road repair or bridge replacement. To Lewis, the new sheriff, it was a necessary protection to buy the time needed to get things under control. How much it would buy him, he didn't know. A few locals used the old grown-over logging roads to make an escape, but they knew enough to not tell.

While most of the residents of Miller's Crossing remained in hiding, unless they needed to go out, a few attempted to take a stand once their fear dissipated. Lewis had used emergency alert programs set up after 9/11 to send a specific order to every member of the town. That message stated: "Do not attempt to confront these creatures. Stay inside." Most heeded it; some did not. They headed out in patrols just after dusk, armed with whatever they had on hand: everything from hunting rifles, to farming tools, to a few homemade Molotov cocktails. Their goal was to take back their town. Their achievement was adding to the loss-of-life total.

Jacob could see the fires they set with their attacks from the window of his father's hospital room. Edward had not moved or spoken since that day. Every doctor in town took a shot at reviewing his condition. Each left scratching their head, no closer to the cause of his condition or a treatment to bring him around. Jacob had only left a few times during that time; once to take a walk and try to clear his head, which didn't work. There was a constant something there; what, he didn't really know. He mentioned it to Father Murray once, who explained it was probably him sensing the ghosts and demons that now roamed openly around town. That was possible. He had felt it a few times at first, but it had come and gone. Now it stayed and never left.

The other time he left his father's side was a move of honorable intent but foolhardy execution. Lewis had just left his father's room after receiving a radio call about another raiding party attempting to confront several demons around Westside Park, just under a mile away from the hospital. Jacob heard him order Tony to stop them before he rushed out himself to help intervene. The response from Tony told him that Sarah was with them. To Jacob's knowledge, that was only the second time she had left the shed since all this started. No one had talked to him directly about everything they knew, or had they? He had to hope they knew more about what was going on than they told him, which was nothing. What was clear was she was the key at the center of all this. If he could get through to her, he could put a stop to it, a thought he considered rather deeply as possibly the last thought his father had before what happened to him.

He ventured out and saw a sight that beat any horror film he watched late on Friday and Saturday nights. Animal-like beasts walked around on two legs, screaming, howling, and snorting. Their claws scratched against the concrete of the sidewalk in ominous screeches. At the center, his sister. Still dressed in what she wore the last time he saw her, that was all he recognized. Her eyes were wide and solid white. A cape of raven hair flew around behind her as she floated down the road and up into the park. Her arms and hands directed the creatures without a sound. They maintained a ring around her. One he couldn't find a way through. He watched as the raiding party rounded the corner, firing their rifles at the creatures. A few rushed at them, swinging axes and machetes. The flails were wild and only connected a few times, not that it made any difference. They brushed the attacks off like gnats on a summer afternoon.

Lewis's voice echoed through the loudspeaker on top of Tony's cruiser. "Stop and disperse, for your own safety." He repeated it over and over again above the screaming, but it was too late. Those were not from the creatures. They were from the men who attacked them. As a last gasp attempt, one man threw a flaming bottle at Sarah. It hit and exploded around her, but not on her. Inside that sphere of flames, her skin changed. Marks and symbols pressed through her skin from the inside while her lips moved. With a single flip of her hand, she sent those flames back at the attacker, Clay Harris. The ball of flame lifted him off the ground and up into the sky, like a shooting star rising from the ground, and he disappeared from view. Then, without warning or cause, she disappeared too, just as she had the first time she emerged from the shed. Jacob could only assume she returned to it like she had before.

That trip was last night. Lewis saw him and caught up with him halfway back to the hospital. Jacob wasn't running back like he had on his way out. Instead, he was walking, defeated, and exposed. Lewis gathered him into Tony's patrol car. There was no grand lecture on how stupid he was for doing this. Jacob merely sat in the back and cried. When he went out, he wanted to help but didn't know how. Seeing her like that cemented in him how hopeless the situation was. That was no longer his sister. She was something different. Evil. The destroyer of the world she had become part of over the last few years. Her actions killed people she had grown to call friends and family, and she didn't even hesitate. Look what she had done to her own father.

When Tony dropped Jacob and Lewis back off at the hospital, they walked in through the emergency room. Each bay around them was full of victims from tonight's encounters, either from the raiding party or those who were caught outside after dark. The fate of the victims was already sealed. That didn't stop the medical staff from trying to save them. This was a nightly occurrence.

Back up in Edward's room, Lewis called in Wendy Tolliver and placed Jacob in her care under "house arrest." Her instructions were to not let Jacob go anywhere, which she hadn't. Every time he shifted in the chair or got up to walk around the room, she took a position at the door. Even when he walked down to take a shower, she walked by his side the whole way like she was escorting a prisoner to lockup. If he had any other plans to leave, it would have to be out the window. Not an option from four stories up.

2

Jacob's excursion was not tiring physically, but it exhausted him on an emotional level, adding to the stress and strain that had built up inside him over the last week. He had spent days fighting back his body's need. A few times it won, but not for more than a few moments of respite. Each time, he shook awake to check on his dad when he realized what had happened. This time, his mind and body both gave in to the need. His head dipped once, then pulled up. Then it bobbed again. The final surrender was when his shoulders slouched, and he slid down in the chair. The mostly quiet room around him went from a place of frantic movement that appeared full of chaos to one that slid softly into a world of darkness.

The tranquil darkness didn't last. The something that had been there in his mind when this all started was still there, and it grew. It became heavier, but was familiar. It wasn't long before the darkness melted away, leaving Jacob in his room back at the family home. Something wasn't right though. It wasn't his room now. A blank wall was where his flat-screen television hung. The drapes were something straight out of some old sitcom from the eighties. He ripped them down the first day he was in that room, which explained the musky smell and the lack of anything in the room. The room was how he first saw it when he walked in through the door, which was where he now stood.

He turned around and looked down the stairs to the living room. It was much the same. Old console television against the wall. The same brown-and-orange sofa that greeted them when they walked in. A simple green loop rug under the dusty coffee table. As he descended further, the dining room looked like it did then and now. They hadn't made many changes in that room. Jacob continued walking around the house, but having accepted that this was the day they moved in, seeing everything as it was no longer surprised him. What he was looking for now was his family.

He ducked back upstairs to check his father's room. The door was closed, which it was on that day. After that, his father had always kept it open unless he was in there. Jacob turned the handle and opened it, slowly, timidly. With it cracked open, he poked his head inside. It was all wrong. This wasn't his father's room. It was the hospital room, his father still lying in the bed connected to a ventilator. Father Murray was asleep in the chair by the bed. Wendy Tolliver sat in a guest chair, her neck craned almost straight up to see the television attached to the wall. Next to her on the other side of the hospital bed was Jacob, slouched down in the chair. Each frozen in time. Not even the image on the television screen moved. He walked around and waved his hand in front of Wendy's face, but she didn't flinch. Then out of an abundance of curiosity, he walked over to himself slouched in the chair. His hand shook as he reached toward himself and then paused just above his arm. *What would happen if I touch it?* he thought. There was only one way to find out. He started to lower his hand the remaining few inches, but held up. There was something eerie about this, almost morbid. The sound of his breathing grew rapid and shallow as he extended his fingers the last bit and touched his left forearm lightly. He leapt back as the hair on his left arm stood on end and he felt the pressure of someone touching him. With a racing heart, and fear of what he didn't understand running through his mind, Jacob backed out of the room and into the hallway. The bedroom door slammed behind him, without him pulling it closed.

Across the hall stood another closed door. That was not unusual. It was Sarah's room, and she only left her door open when she wasn't home. Something about needing her privacy and having an annoying younger brother. Even as Jacob got older, it didn't change, but the time she spent in the room did. Instead of staying locked behind the door from sunup to sundown, she spent more time downstairs in the living room or sitting at the kitchen table up against the window, reading. He reached forward for her door handle and gave it a turn. It turned easily and opened. A gust of air sucked in and pulled the door handle from his grasp, sending the door slamming backward into the doorstop on the wall. The room itself was empty. None of her furniture was in there. Just a layer of dust that rose off the floor with the gust and created a cloud in the center of the room that danced in the light coming in through the window. Jacob stepped in to grab the door handle and close it, but walked into a tempest of air that pushed against his upper body and pinned him against the doorframe. It took every ounce of strength he could strain out of his seventeen-year-old athletic frame to push with both hands against the doorjamb. The shove sent him out backward, crashing into the door of his father's room. Then Sarah's door exploded shut. The window blew the hair on his head backward.

With no one upstairs, he continued his search downstairs. The living and dining rooms were both empty. A push through the door to the kitchen found a familiar scene. Sarah was sitting there, in the breakfast nook next to the window, reading. The focus of her concentration was the same little simple brown leather book his father carried around with him everywhere. She didn't acknowledge him as he entered the kitchen, and appeared frozen like those he found in his father's bedroom. He took a few more steps toward her, and her right hand jerked up and held up a palm to tell him to stop. Her face turned sideways, giving Jacob an unimpeded view of her profile. It was her again, not the white-eyed marked-up creature he saw earlier that night. She was reading, quickly, but her mouth made no sound.

She put the book down and turned toward him. Eyes cold and hostile. An expression on her face that leered whilst also attempting to be friendly. "Hey, little brother," she said. It was her voice, loud and clear, but at the same time, it wasn't. The same tone and tenor, but lacking any of the personality and warmth.

"Sarah?" he asked, unsure if it was really her or some figment in a dream.

"In the flesh." Her cold blue eyes watched as he walked around the island in the kitchen and closer to the table. They didn't blink as Jacob took the unnecessary path. He wanted to see how she reacted. To size her up.

"Is this really you?" he asked, and then felt foolish about it. If this was a dream, what answer other than yes would his mind give to itself? Then he wondered, had he ever had a dream in which he knew he was dreaming?

"Yes, Jacob. It's me. It's really me," she said as she stood up from the table and walked toward him, arms outstretched for an embrace.

Jacob stepped backward to avoid her, and her arms dropped by her sides.

"I understand. A lot has happened."

"What did you do to Dad?" demanded Jacob.

"You don't need to worry about him. He is fine. I did it to protect him. This... this thing in me wanted to kill him. If I didn't do this, he would be dead."

"What thing? What are you talking about, Sarah?"

"There is something, or someone, in me. It's hard to explain. It has been here for years, since the Reaping. For a long time, it was gone, but a few weeks back, it pushed me aside and took over. Jacob, I am not in control of my body. Not in control of my life. I can see what happens, but I can't do anything. When I try, it about kills me. Like with Dad, and with you tonight."

"Tonight, what do you mean tonight?" roared Jacob. His neck tensed and fists clenched.

"I saw you. It saw you, and it wanted to hurt you. I did what I could to hurt it to keep it from hurting you."

Hearing she could hurt it gave him an idea. "You got to stop this, Sarah. People are dying. Fight it," Jacob implored.

"I can't. It's too strong. You don't understand."

She was right, Jacob didn't understand. He still didn't know what the "it" she spoke of was. He wasn't sure if this was real or just some construct of his physically and emotionally exhausted subconscious. In fact, that made more sense than this being real. How could she be here talking to him?

"You don't understand," she continued in a mumble. Her hands covered her face, and it appeared she began to sob.

"Sarah, I don't know what this is, but tell me how to help you."

"You can't," she said.

"Is this real? Are you here talking to me?" he asked, once again feeling foolish at asking such a question.

She looked up from her hands and answered, tears streaming down her face, "Yes, Jacob, this is real. The abilities I have... the abilities I have through it let me reach out and talk to you like this. I know right now you're asleep in a chair next to Dad. I'm sitting in the shed in the woods, where it retreated when I struck out at it to save you. I can't do much more than that."

"I am coming for you!" he vowed. "As soon as I'm awake, I am coming for you."

"No! Don't!" she shrieked. "It will kill you! Stay away! Keep everyone away!" She reached out and grabbed his arms at the elbow. Her touch burned and seared the skin, causing him to pull back. The pain stopped, but gray smoke rose from soot stains on his arms. Just before he yanked away, her face changed. The shape, the color, the presence of her was evil and ominous. Yellow and red replaced the blue of her eyes. Pits of black replaced the whites. A smell of death and decay accompanied her voice. "Jacob, you can't help me."

"The cross" he whispered to himself.

Sarah heard it too. "Not even that. Dad had that in his hand when he tried." Her voice trembled, and she looked around behind her. "I gotta go."

"Sarah, tell me how to help you. There has to be a way."

"No, Jacob. I gotta go."

She frantically ran toward the back door and fumbled with the door handle. She attempted again and didn't turn it far enough before yanking on it. Finally, the door opened a crack and then stopped and slammed. Her shoulders were hunched with her head down as she turned back toward Jacob and rushed him. Strange markings, etched from the inside, scarred her skin. Yellow pupils glowed against the black pits that surrounded them. She grabbed his arms with claws.

Jacob tried to pull away but couldn't. The sharp claws dug into his skin as its evil gaze studied him. Then, with the voice of a thousand tortured souls, it screamed at him. Jacob felt something draining from him. His heart pounded in his chest as his breath left his lungs. Then something else was leaving him. He couldn't put his finger on what it was, but he was losing focus, losing himself. A white light emerged from his body. Small particles traced the path around him and then out toward Sarah. The more particles he saw, the weaker he felt. He was fading, and he knew it.

"NO!" screamed his sister's voice. It echoed around him as the claws let go, letting him fall.

Jacob landed in his chair in the hospital room. Heart still pounding and out of breath, he startled awake and stood straight up.

"You okay, Jake?" asked Wendy. "You have a bad dream?" she asked before he answered her first question. "You aren't the only one. We are all living in one right now. You're safe."

Jacob looked at his father lying still in the bed. His own hands subconsciously rubbed his arms. The area around his elbows was tender, and he rolled up the sleeves of his black sweatshirt. There were scratches and soot marks on both.

3

The first light of day cracked through the window and across the room, but the scene inside stayed the same as it had for the last seven mornings. Edward remained motionless in the hospital bed. Air cycled in and out of his lungs with the help of tubes. The rhythmic pump of the machine was no longer noticeable. It was just part of the essence of the room. Father Murray was still asleep in the recliner. He hadn't stirred much in the last several hours. Only a few snorts and moans in his sleep. Jacob was awake to hear them. His sleep came in fits. Here and there. Each time, he woke startled and searched his thoughts for any more conversations with Sarah that might have occurred while he was asleep. Nothing. Only the marks on the inside of his elbows told him it was real.

Despite the gloomy surroundings, it was a beautiful day. Cool and crisp, not a cloud in the sky. From the fourth-floor window, Jacob could see the majestic reds and oranges of fall. Out there, people should have been preparing for the great fall traditions like the carnival at the elementary school, and Halloween. Thoughts of costumes and apple bobbing should be on the mind of every child in Miller's Crossing. Instead they were trapped in their homes, while real spooks roamed the streets. Their parents only risked leaving on quick trips for the necessary supplies. From this view, though, everything looked like a normal fall day.

Jacob continued to look out the window upon the town. It was a break, one his eyes and mind needed. Once his eyes took it, the nagging concern that he might miss his father move or something consumed his mind. The thought ate at him and then became a repeated phrase over and over in his head. After enough time, the weight of the words stacked up, one on top of the other, so much he had to turn around and check on his father, just long enough to clear the thought. Then it was back to the window.

He was lost in the beauty. His mind flew like a bird across the treetops as his tired soul drifted into a daydream. The thoughts of what was behind him in the room faded. It was peaceful but brief. In the distance, screaming down Main Street, were the unmistakable flashing blue lights of a patrol car. Were they running a siren? Jacob couldn't tell from inside, but he doubted it. That would be foolish. First, who was on the road that they needed to get out of the way? Second, why attract the attention of those beasts?

With Wendy in the room behind him, watching to make sure he didn't sneak out again, it meant that was Terrance or Tony. The only remaining deputies. Jacob watched as it continued, disappearing behind trees and buildings for a few moments only to reappear. Then it turned down Oak Drive toward the hospital. The leaves of the great oaks the street was named for were all over the ground, giving him an unobstructed view through the barren branches. It was not going at high speed, just a normal drive with lights.

At the entrance to the hospital, it pulled in. That was not much of a shock to Jacob. It would only be logical for the hospital to be one of a few destinations. The first thought that exploded into his mind was that someone was hurt. He stood up to look down through the window and watch the car maneuver through the parking lot and toward the emergency services entrance, but it didn't. Instead of taking the left it needed to make, it took a right toward the main entrance.

Jacob watched as long as he could from his perch in the window. The car disappeared behind the ledge and around the corner. The flashing blue lights reflected off the cars in the lot, but even that eventually disappeared. With the curiosity gone and the fascination with the landscape subsided, he returned to his post of the last eight days and sat watching his father, with only a few glances up at the national morning news show on the television.

They were going on and on about the latest proposed stimulus bill going through the senate. One side was accusing the other of holding it up, but they had yet to request a vote. Jacob had no interest or stomach for politics. It appeared his grandfather had tinkered with it at the local level at some point, but what he saw in the old news clippings was different from this. He got things done, or tried to. From his view, no matter how many times his father tried to describe the artistry of the modern political system, it was just a bunch of old people who never learned how to share in the sandbox in kindergarten. His attention was waning when Lewis Tillingsly walked in, a familiar black hat on his head, minus the star that used to adorn it. Keeping with the old traditions, the hat was off his head before he entered the room. He held it low at his waist as he paid respects to Wendy, Jacob, and then to Edward, who wasn't in any shape to return them.

"Any change?" he asked.

Jacob just shook his head, looking glum.

"Chin up," Lewis said. "He's a fighter." Then he walked toward Father Murray, still asleep in the recliner next to the bed. He tapped the father on the shoulder, but he only rustled a bit to move away from the disturbance. This time, he reached down and shook his shoulder ever so lightly. The eyes of the old priest sprang open and searched around the room, settling on Lewis standing over him.

"Father, your guest is here," Lewis said.

The vinyl of the recliner gave a ripping sound as Father Murray hurried to his feet, and the material released its hold on the fabric of his black slacks and coat. He quickly adjusted his clothing with a tug here and a tuck there while he followed Lewis out of the room. Jacob watched as they both left without explanation. He didn't really need one. Seeing the patrol car arrive just moments ago, and now the announcement of a visitor, Jacob could piece the puzzle together, at least partially. Who the visitor was remained a mystery.

Lewis and Father Murray had been gone for over an hour when Wendy got up and announced, "I need some coffee. Want something?"

Jacob just shook his head, which provoked a concerned look on Wendy's face.

"You haven't eaten or slept much since all this happened. Why don't I walk down to the cafeteria and get you some eggs and toast?" She continued to look at him.

Jacob knew she would not take no for an answer, so he nodded, which caused her to smile for a second or two before she headed out.

Jacob was hungry, and he could think of worse things to eat, but that wasn't the driving motivation. This gave him a few minutes without the watchful eye of his guard, who hadn't left him since Lewis asked her to keep an eye on him. She hadn't even left to call home or anything, which Jacob thought was odd at first. With everything going on, you would worry about what was happening with your family. An exchange he overheard between Wendy and Father Murray explained it. The father was helping her pray and consoling her for the loss of her husband, Daniel, who had been a member of Marcus's search party. Jacob immediately felt bad. He was dead because of them—or Sarah, to be more precise. The feeling lessened as he realized she didn't appear to hold any ill will toward him or his father. She was compassionate toward them both, not something that was just a professional duty.

It was only a moment after the sound of Wendy's hard-soled shoes disappeared down the vinyl-tiled hall before Jacob was out of his chair and slinking toward the door. He stood there for a second just listening for anyone approaching. Once he was satisfied there was no one coming, he stuck his head out the door and looked around. The hall was vacant and plain; the wall color matched the floor. Only a single nurse sat behind the nurses' station, clear at the other end of the hall. At the end in the other direction was a single atrium, or so they called it. It wasn't much more than a room in the corner of the building. Windows covered the exterior walls. A simple sectional sofa that had seen better days sat under the windows. Used mostly by family members who needed to take a call in private or just a moment to gather their thoughts while visiting a loved one.

The room was occupied, as it often was, and the occupants resembled some that Jacob believed would be in there if they were delivering grim news to a family, but he knew that not to be the case. He knew two of the men and slightly recognized the third. The tall slender figure in all black wearing a black wide-brimmed hat, like the one Father Murray wore, had first visited them eight years ago.

4

The hallway remained empty, as was much of the hospital. It was a small, square building. Five floors in total, with the emergency room and several doctors' offices on the first floor. A couple of surgical suites were on the second floor, where the most common surgery was the removal of tonsils from a child with a sore throat. The recovery and medical rooms were on the third and fourth floors. They reserved the top floor for the administrative offices. On any given day there were only twenty or so patients in the complex. They referred most serious medical issues to a larger city such as Richmond where the facilities were more capable. The only exceptions were emergencies where the doctors at County General stabilized the patient while they awaited an airlift to arrive to transport them.

"Jacob, you can come on in here," said Lewis Tillingsly.

Jacob had snuck down the hallway as far as he dared to hear what the three men were talking about. His attempt to stay hidden had failed. He crept into the room, not sure what he was walking in on. All three men watched as he entered. Their gazes made him uncomfortable, but he didn't understand why. They were not leering, but looking at him with a great deal of curiosity.

Inside the door, he stood face-to-face with the tall slender man he spied from down the hall. Father Lucian stepped forward and extended his hand. In his thick accent he said, "A pleasure to see you again, Jacob. I am sorry it is under such circumstances."

Jacob shook the Italian man's hand. The first time he saw Father Lucian was about eight years ago when he stood outside their home waiting for his father. The man stood next to Father Murray as they pulled up in front. He didn't have an opportunity to talk to him much then. His father sent him and Sarah inside. After that night, they had just a brief exchange of "Nice to meet you, young man," before he left. The next time was not for another five years, when he flew over to pick up Sarah for her training. At that time, Jacob had just started to feel what his father and sister did. Father Lucian took a few minutes to talk to Jacob. His words stuck with him. "Don't be afraid of this. Embrace it. Enjoy it and live it. Your time will come soon enough."

"It's good to see you too," Jacob said. "Can you help?"

The two priests shared a look between themselves at the question. Both men looked concerned, which caused a stir in that dark pit that had settled in Jacob over the past week.

He studied each for any visual tell, but neither gave much, so he demanded again, "Can you help? You have to."

"Jacob," Father Murray started. "We will do everything we can. It's very complicated. First, we need to understand what *this* is."

"You don't know what this is? This is a possession. Like in the movies. Can't you go out and do some kind of exorcism or something and end all this?" exploded Jacob, eyes bulging and fists clenched at his sides.

"I would agree, it is a possession," said Father Lucian.

"Jacob, possessions are very difficult situations to deal with. Hollywood makes you think you sprinkle some holy water on the person, say a few prayers, and once the demon says its name, that is it, it is all over and the person gets up and walks away. It is nothing like that," explained Father Murray.

"Absolutely not. The last possession I interceded with took over three months to finally free the person, and they still aren't who they were before. But that was nothing like this. That was just a normal person who suffered from symptoms some might relate to mental illness," said Father Lucian.

"This is an all-out assault. Something that has never happened before," Father Murray added.

"Indeed, and never involving one of our own," Father Lucian said.

"What does that mean? Assault? Is this a war?"

"Yes, a war from the start of time that will continue until the end of time," said Father Lucian. "That is why they picked this place. Your sister might have just been... well, how would you say? A lucky convenience."

Father Murray invited Jacob to have a seat on the worn sofa that lined the wall. Even though it was now fall, the sun still made it up high during the middle of the day. This allowed the radiant heat to more than peer in through the windows of the sunroom, heating the cloth cushions of the ratty old green sofa. The warmth of the cushion was a welcome sensation to Jacob. The hospital itself remained rather chilly around the clock.

Over the next hour, Fathers Murray and Lucian explained to Jacob many things his father had already talked to him about. In particular, what was special about Miller's Crossing and why a demon would pick this location. They also explained what "sensitives" and "keepers" were. Both were terms he had never heard his father use. When Father Lucian explained that their family were keepers, he felt a tinge of something special. They explained that no keeper had ever been compromised before.

"Then how did this happen?" asked Jacob.

That question caused Father Murray to look down at the floor before taking a seat next to Jacob. He looked deep into the young man's eyes and explained. "I let the demon in, over thirty years ago. Something I have regretted every day since." The solemn tone in his voice continued throughout the entire explanation, which started with the day the demon killed Jacob's grandparents and ended on the football field on the night the locals call the Reaping. One detail about that night that Jacob didn't know until now was that the demon, Abaddon, had targeted Sarah before his father confronted it and sent it fleeing, or so they thought.

"I now believe it attached itself to her then, and *that* explains why she was so strong. Her abilities were beyond any we had seen from any other keeper before," interjected Father Lucian.

"So, you caused all this?" asked Jacob. There was an edge to his voice and an increase in the tension of his body. Jacob was an even-tempered kid, never losing his temper when his sister kidded him or he didn't get his way. Not to say he never got mad, he just never lost it. Never really had a teenage hormone-driven outburst, that he could remember, but this was close and getting closer. It was building up, and it wouldn't be long before it exploded.

Before the anger could boil any further, Lewis stepped in. "Now is not the time to rehash old wounds. Your father and Father Murray have already settled things. What is important is to handle what is here now. Fathers, do you have any ideas?"

"I need to see it," said Father Lucian.

Stunned looks appeared on everyone who heard the sentence.

5

"I'm going on record right now, I am completely against this," Lewis Tillingsly said. His arms crossed as he stood in front of Tony's cruiser. They had parked the black-and-white Impala at the same location every day, and most nights, since it began. He only left when the creatures Lewis assigned him to monitor left and headed somewhere in town. When they did, he followed them at a safe distance, reporting in and helping to keep others out of their way.

"He will be safe. You have my word," Father Lucian said.

"Can you even guarantee your own safety? We all saw what she did to Edward," insisted Lewis. Jacob saw his eyes dart to him when he said "she."

"I can take care of myself," Jacob said. He tried to sound confident, but inside he was a bundle of nerves on a roller coaster. How could he make such a claim when he still didn't know what this was?

"I have to agree with Lewis. We have both been out there." Father Murray provided the final vote that put an end to the discussion, and Father Lucian nodded in agreement.

Jacob considered protesting, but he knew it would be fruitless. Also, inside, a large part of him urged him to stay quiet. The fear of what was out there had taken hold, overriding his decisions. He still had seen nothing beyond what he did last night in the park, but he felt it. It had been there a week. Now, being this close to it, it was overwhelming.

From a safe distance, Jacob watched as the tall and slender priest turned away from the four men who stood at the front of the patrol car, and walked along the double yellow line down Harper Hill Road and across the bridge that spanned Walter's Creek. Each stride was the same pace and length as the previous. A board-straight back and shoulders exuded confidence as he made his approach. Once over the bridge, he stopped and pivoted at a right angle to the road and stepped across the lane. There was a brief pause when his black leather shoes hit the white line that marked the edge of the road.

A single foot raised up and stepped forward off the tarmac and onto the grass of the shoulder. At that moment, a large rumble sent Jacob and the others scurrying back behind the car. The ground didn't shake. This rumble resembled the deep throaty growl of gigantic beast. His view from his new perch was blocked, and he stood up to see Father Lucian. The ground under them was still not shaking, and the rumble had stopped several seconds earlier, but Jacob's legs felt like rubber bands. His hands braced himself against the trunk deck.

Father Lucian was unaffected and statue-straight and stiff, one foot on the shoulder, the other still on the tarmac. The second foot lifted and joined the other on the grass. Another rumble, this time louder, raced at them from the grove of trees that stood tall and strong in the center of the desolate landscape. Jacob leaned onto the car and kept his eyes on Father Lucian. The roar raised dust as it raced outward and past him. His pants legs and jacket flapped violently in the wind, but he didn't surrender any ground.

What happened next sent a shiver down Jacob like he had never felt before. Not even the death of his mother shocked him like this. He was now thankful that Lewis and Father Murray didn't let him join Father Lucian. When the gust passed by, Father Lucian took another step toward the woods. There was no roar this time in response to the step. Instead, every sliver of debris, from the smallest piece of sawdust to a branch several feet long, shot up from their resting place on the ground and hovered head high. The layer pulsated like a great ocean with waves of peaks and valleys.

On his rubber legs, Jacob walked around the cruiser to get a better view of the scene. His entire body trembled at the sight. For as far as he could see, it was the same thing. Then he looked down the road at Father Lucian, who still hadn't yielded. The priest took off his black wide-brimmed hat and carefully bent down to place it on the ground next to him. Then he stood back up, again straight and strong. His left hand reached into his coat and retrieved an object that he placed on his head. The distance and remnants of the dust cloud created by the first roar clouded Jacob's vision, and he couldn't see exactly what the object was. Father Lucian stepped forward, and the debris parted around him. As he moved in further, Jacob lost sight of him as the debris closed in around him. All they could do was wait.

And wait they did. First thirty minutes, then an hour. Dark shadows of late afternoon crept onto their position. With it, the chill of fall and a realization that Tony was the first to bring up. "What if he doesn't make it back? Are we going in there to get him?"

Lewis gave a quick shake of his head as he stared at his watch.

Jacob searched the dark feeling that had been with him for the last week for any change. Any sense of a decrease in its intensity that might signal Father Lucian had some effect. There wasn't. Nor was it stronger. There was no change, not that he was sure this was how it even worked. It was all a guess to him at this point. He wasn't even sure this feeling was related to any of this. So many emotions stirred in his head at the moment, Jacob wasn't sure what was what.

Another thirty minutes passed, and the mood of the group took another dip. Jacob had walked as far the bridge over Walter's Creek to get a better view. He searched for any sign that Father Lucian was returning. Behind him, Father Murray now sat in the patrol car, and Tony and Lewis stood quietly outside. They batted about the question Tony had asked earlier a few more times among them. It wasn't until the last time, just over five minutes ago, that Lewis put a timetable on it. They would wait an hour after the fall of darkness and then return to the safety of the police station. Tony would stay behind in case Father Lucian returned.

Darkness fell, and there was still no sign of his return. Jacob stood on top of the bridge where he had for the last hour. Now he was shrouded in complete darkness. Only the lights from Lewis's large Plymouth and Tony's patrol cruiser cast light on him from behind. His shadow stretched from the bridge down the center of Harper Hill Road and to the spot Father Lucian turned into the woods from. The darkness also blocked out the scene of horror that was to his right. It was still there, he didn't doubt that. Just couldn't see it, which, with the dead silence that surrounded them, made it that much eerier.

After another forty minutes, the mechanical crank and firing of an older eight-cylinder big block broke the silence. It stuttered at first as it warmed up after the cold start. Jacob knew what this meant. They would leave shortly. His heart sank when he thought Father Lucian would just be another statistic added to the body count. A count that his family was responsible for. No matter how many ways he tried to think about it, he couldn't avoid that fact. They were responsible for everything that had happened. Directly, with Sarah at the center of it, but also indirectly. As Father Lucian explained to him earlier, it was their responsibility as keepers to protect this location, and they failed.

Jacob turned to walk back toward the car, but before he completed the turn, something appeared down the road in the headlights. Whatever it was slowly emerged out of the shadows and onto the road surface. His mind finally recognized the form and took off running toward it. To his right, there was a thunderous crash. A gust of dust rushed at him. He could only assume the objects that had been hanging in the air most of the afternoon had finally fallen back to the ground. It wasn't something he gave too much thought to. His attention was on the individual that crawled out on the road on their hands and knees and now collapsed.

When he finally reached them, he recognized it was Father Lucian. He was barely conscious and in obvious pain. A crimson curtain of blood poured down his face. The blood oozed from punctures that lined his forehead. His white eyes looked up through the curtain at Jacob, while his body shook.

6

Jacob followed Father Murray and Lewis Tillingsly as far as they would allow, but as soon as they pulled the green curtain shut around the emergency room bay, he could follow them no further. Behind the curtain, doctors tended to Father Lucian. He was still conscious but in immense pain. Deep scratches covered his body. They were in rows of three. Each oozed blood. With every movement as they loaded him in and out of the back of Lewis's car, he'd screamed and writhed in pain. His left hand grabbed at the sources of his pain, a crown of thorns clutched tightly in his right hand that neither Father Murray nor the nurses that met them at the door could pry out.

The moans and screams that emerged from behind the curtain were horrifying and blood curdling. The dread that had consumed Jacob for the last several days descended further down into the depths of despair. So many had been hurt and lost, and now another lay behind the curtain. As the pain-filled sounds stopped, and the parade of nurses and doctors ceased, Jacob assumed the worst. When Father Murray emerged and pulled the curtain back, Jacob felt an explosion of relief. Behind the curtain was Father Lucian, sitting up in the bed. Bandages covered the exposed areas of his body, but he was up, alert, and talking with Lewis and a doctor. His expression looked to be that of a man in good humor, not one in pain. His right hand still hung on to the crown of thorns tightly. It seemed to glow slightly. Something Jacob attributed to the lights that hung over the bed.

"All right, Father, I am a believer," said the tall doctor in green scrubs. He passed Father Murray as he exited through the gap in the curtain. Father Murray appeared to smirk at that revelation.

"Is he okay?" Jacob asked.

"Oh yes, and getting better all the time. His faith is healing him," Father Murray said and then pointed to the man's right hand.

"That is a relic? Like the cross?"

"Jacob, that is not any relic. That is the crown of thorns that Jesus wore when he was crucified. It is the most sacred of all. That is why Father Lucian wields it."

"The one?" Jacob asked. The revelation that his father possessed a cross made from the crucifix was hard enough to swallow. It had taken him a few days until he was brave enough to pick it up and hold it. Each time he did, he treated it as an antique, holding it on top of his open palm. Never brave enough to close his hand around it. The fear of dropping it and it shattering on the ground was ever present in his thoughts, even though he had seen his father and Sarah deposit it rather harshly on a table from time to time without damage. Now he found himself in the presence of the actual crown of thorns that was depicted in every image of the crucifixion. He took a step backward to give it more space.

"Father, a little help please..." Lewis called from inside the curtained area.

Jacob turned his attention from Father Murray and back to the hospital bed, where Father Lucian was attempting to stand up and get dressed. Father Murray rushed to the side of his bed and looked for an unbandaged area to grab hold of and restrain him in the bed, but every surface was covered.

Father Murray pleaded, "Lucian, please. Stay still. You have been through a lot."

"Nonsense," he said as he stood up beside the bed.

Lewis stood there with his arms out to catch the battered priest, but he was steady as a rock on his feet. Not a wobble or waver. He brushed away his attempt to assist with his left hand. Then he reached over and grabbed the bandage that covered his right forearm.

"Leave it alone, Francesco, please," Father Murray pleaded again. The last syllable wasn't out of his mouth before the bandage was dangling by a bit of adhesive tape. The flesh of his forearm completely exposed, only three red scratches remained where enormous chunks of flesh had been missing before. The scratches faded by the second, right in front of Jacob's eyes.

The remaining bandages were removed with care, the last of them coming off as a nurse walked back in to check on the patient. Shock was written all over her face and in her eyes as she saw the pile of bandages on the hospital bed, and the man brought in on the brink of death just half an hour ago now standing and adjusting his black hat.

Father Lucian walked out of the area and past the nurse, who stood there with her mouth wide open. "Thank you for the wonderful care," he said.

"His faith healed him," Father Murray said as they passed her.

All she could say in response was, "I see."

Lewis followed Fathers Murray and Lucian, Jacob falling in behind them, back outside. A light rain shower had started when they were inside, driving the chill that accompanied the late hour on this fall evening. Jacob shoved his hands as far as he could into the pockets of his jeans. The nip still bit at him through the sleeves of his sweatshirt.

"Father, do you mind if we retire to the church to talk?" asked Father Lucian.

"Not at all. We can set you up in the guest room."

"Father, why don't you two go ahead," Lewis said. "Jacob and I will retrieve Father Lucian's bags from upstairs and be along shortly."

"All right. My car is over this way," Father Murray said, and he and Father Lucian walked out into the gloomy night.

Lewis headed back upstairs to Jacob's father's room. Jacob just followed blindly. He knew the way like the back of his hand now, but that wasn't it. His mind was elsewhere. It struggled with what he had just seen. The stories he had heard his father and Father Murray tell talked of amazing events. Some he had just begun to accept as real, and others he accepted as just that, stories. This was the first time he had seen anything like this with his own eyes.

When they got up to the room, Wendy was still at her post in the chair, watching TV. Jacob looked at his father for any sign that something had changed, but to his disappointment, there was nothing. His father lay there just like he had for the last several days. Arms and legs showing no signs of moving or even adjusting to get more comfortable.

"Anything?" Lewis asked Wendy.

"Nah, he has been quiet. Not a movement or sound," she reported as she looked back at Jacob's father with a look of disappointment. Then she looked at Jacob with a half-smile and mouthed, "Sorry."

"Take the night off and go get some sleep. I got junior. He won't be giving me any trouble," said Lewis.

There was no hesitation or question if he was sure. Wendy grabbed her purse and jacket and headed out. Jacob saw her give Edward one last look before she exited the room.

"Jake, grab the father's bags and let's go before it gets too late."

Without a word, Jacob grabbed the two simple black leather bags, both tattered and well worn but still sturdy as he picked them up. From their weight, Jacob could imagine what was in both bags. One probably had a night shirt and a single change of clothes. The other had objects that shifted around more. Probably toiletries, and the larger item he felt move as he lifted it might be another pair of shoes.

On the drive over, Jacob's thoughts continued to stay focused on what he had witnessed. He was a believer in the spiritual. He had to be with the life they lived, but this was beyond that. This was biblical. This was something the best screenwriter wouldn't dream up. He struggled. He struggled a great and deal and finally opened up.

"Mr. Tillingsly, how did Father Lucian heal so fast?"

There was a big gulp followed by a cough from the man who sat in the driver's seat of the car. He stumbled and stammered for a few seconds before he finally said, "Jacob, I am not really sure. I know what we saw, and based on things I have seen with your grandfather and your dad, there are two explanations I can offer. Sometimes, a demon does something that is just temporary. Like a wasp stinging you if you get too close to their hive. That is the easier explanation, and something I have seen a lot. Then I have seen things that I can't explain. Things that go beyond what I can explain."

"Which do you think this is?" Jacob asked.

"Well, this time I'm not sure. Probably leaning more toward the things-I-can't-explain side. I know what my eyes saw, but my brain can't explain it."

"Same here. I'm still not sure if I saw what I think I did. Maybe my mind was playing tricks on me," Jacob said.

"Jake, buckle up. You're going to experience a lot of that. Sometimes you can't question everything and try to explain it. Sometimes you just have to believe."

7

"How is he doing?" Lewis asked as he walked in through the back screen door of Father Murray's home.

It struck Jacob that with all the time Father Murray was around his family, it was always at their house or the church. He had never been inside Father Murray's house. He also couldn't decide if his surroundings surprised him or not. It was simple. Not overly large-looking from the outside. Inside, the kitchen was just large enough for a single table with four chairs. Neither was particularly fancy, just plain unfinished wood. A single gas stove, not of this decade or the previous one either, with a matching white refrigerator. A white porcelain farmhouse sink sat under the window with bleached white curtains hanging over it.

"Eh, he is doing fine. Just cleaning himself up a bit," Father Murray said. "I'm making some coffee. Would you like some?"

Lewis nodded.

"Jacob, coffee?" he asked.

Jacob shook his head at Father Murray's offer. Coffee was not a taste he had acquired yet. His version of caffeine came in more sugary sources of various colors. Not that he didn't need some. A large yawn was an indicator of that.

Father Murray handed Lewis a cup and then grabbed two more and led them into a dining room. Like the kitchen, it wasn't anything remarkable. Dark wood molding, white walls, and a similar but larger table. Up against the opposite wall sat an old bureau with a large book on top of it. It was open, with an ornate bookmark.

Lewis took a chair on one side, and Father Murray placed a cup in front of one chair and then took the one next to it for himself. Jacob looked around and took the one on the side with Lewis. The sound of water running came from the only two doors in the room. Both doors were open and appeared to lead to bedrooms. Jacob had to assume there was a shared bathroom, something he once heard called a Jack and Jill on a home improvement show his father watched. Behind him, through an archway, was a sitting area. It was too small to truly call a living room, but it had a small sofa and a television. That was not like the appliances he saw in the kitchen. It was a modern high-definition flat-screen. No smaller than fifty-two inches. Not a surprise. The father liked his football, as Jacob heard him and his father talk about on more than one occasion.

"So, what now?" Lewis asked in between sips of his coffee.

Jacob swung his attention to Father Murray to hear the plan but saw only a shrug. That was not the answer he hoped for. He didn't really know what precise answer he hoped for. What to do next escaped him. He had hopes on the drive over that either Father Murray or Lucian would know exactly what to do. Those hopes were a little less than they were earlier in the day. Seeing Father Lucian crawl out to the roadway was a serious blow to them. Now, seeing Father Murray shrug was another serious gut punch.

"Father Lucian said after he cleaned up he would discuss what he saw. I can only hope he has some ideas." Father Murray stopped to take a drink of his coffee. When he placed it back on the table, both hands reached up and made a slow drawn-out rub down the sides of his face. "I don't know what to do next."

The sound of the water stopped, leaving the men in silence, draped under a darkness that covered the whole town. Jacob looked back and forth between the two men at the table with him. Both appeared lost in thought. There was a lot to think about. He knew that. His mind never had a lack of topics to ponder. Front and center were his father and sister. When he wasn't thinking of one, he was thinking of the other. It was his sister he was thinking about when he dipped his head down and laid it on his arms, folded on the table.

Darkness surrounded him. It was peaceful and serene. He knew he was asleep. Exhaustion had gotten the better of him again, and he had nothing in him to fight it. One wonder of the universe that had always fascinated him was how time seemed to stand still while you were asleep. Now when he dreamt, he had a sense of the passage of time, but that was it. When he didn't dream, he closed his eyes and woke up what seemed to be just moments later. It could have been fifteen minutes, an hour, or eight hours. It was always the same. At the moment, he could have been asleep for minutes or hours. He didn't know. There was no dream or anything to give him a sense of time when he heard a voice in the darkness. It cried. No, it sobbed, remorsefully. "Jacob, tell him I am sorry. I couldn't stop it from hurting him."

"Sarah?" he asked.

"Jacob, please. Tell him I am sorry."

"I will," he said, and then a thought hit him. "Or you could tell him yourself. Tell him how to help you."

"Oh no! I couldn't dare," she said. "It would know. It is risky enough to reach out to you."

Hearing her voice sound so lifeless and desperate broke Jacob's heart. He ached as he looked around for any sign of her. There was nothing. Just darkness. The pangs radiated through his subconscious. He needed to see her. To talk to her. To help her.

"Sarah, how can we help you?" he asked.

"You can't," she said.

"There has to be something we can do!" he exclaimed. His own voice echoed in the space. There was no reply. There was nothing. It was different now. He could feel the emptiness. "Sarah!" he cried, but there was no response.

She was gone.

"Sarah, come back. Come back please. Don't go."

A hand shook him on the shoulder with a light touch. Jacob rustled awake and lifted his head. Father Murray was returning to his chair, and the other two men were sitting at the table. Father Lucian sat across from him with a towel around his neck, hair still damp, and a pleasant smile on his face as he gazed at Jacob.

"You were having a dream," said Lewis.

Jacob looked around at the three sets of eyes that looked at him. He had to rub his own to try to clear the blurriness from them. Was it just a dream? He wasn't sure. Probably so. Now that he was awake, it seemed so far away and faded more with every second. "What did I miss?" he asked, his voice still scratchy.

"Not much. Father Lucian just sat down," Lewis said. "So, what happened out there?"

Father Lucian leaned forward and rested his forearms on the table, after a single wipe of the towel across his forehead to take care of drips of water that escaped his hair and headed down his face. "I found the shed. No animals or creatures until I reached it. They were inside with her. Sarah was still there, floating above the symbol, like you said." He gave a simple nod to Father Murray. "It let me walk right in. No resistance at all. It put her and the creatures on display. Like it was proud of what it had done. Proud of what it created. It turned Sarah around for me to see. I saw the girl I remembered, and then I saw a creature in her place with marks that emerged from under her skin. Eyes the blackest black I have ever seen. It was then I felt it probing at me through her glance. Like a punch with a blunt instrument, but in my mind. It tried to enter my thoughts, but it couldn't. Each failure angered it. I could tell. The creatures took notice of my presence. They moved closer to me, growling and snarling the whole time. I felt it try again. That is when I really felt it. It couldn't enter my thoughts, and the entire shed filled with an evil I have never felt before. Even the light of my faith couldn't cut through." He stopped and rubbed his forearms with his hands. It reminded Jacob of how he rubbed his arms once after a pitch on the funny bone beamed him. "One creature dragged me out of the shed and into the woods. The others bit and clawed at me until I was outside the trees. Then I crawled back to the road."

"Do you know what we're dealing with?" asked Father Murray.

Father Lucian's head nodded. "Yes, I know. Not the particular entity or type, but I know what we are dealing with. It is an evil unlike anything we have ever seen before."

8

"So, what now?"

"That, Sheriff, I don't know. It is more than I can handle alone," Father Lucian said.

His voice didn't sound defeated, as Jacob might have believed it would speaking such a statement. There was a sternness to the sound and to his expression. He was a man deep in thought, underneath a great weight. The weight wasn't crushing him. Instead, it caused every step to be measured and careful. Inside, that gave Jacob hope. That hope contrasted with what little patience his teenage emotions could muster at the moment. There was a need to explode at any second and demand to know what they could do.

The only things stopping it were the expressions plastered on the faces of the others at the table. They were defeated. Each searched Father Lucian for hope. Whether they found it, Jacob couldn't be sure. He only glanced at them as he kept his focus looking for his own hope, to quell the eruption brewing.

"I hate to ask this," said Sheriff Tillingsly, "but is there any way to contain it?"

Father Murray and Father Lucian shared a look.

"If we can't get rid of it, our next priority needs to be protecting the town."

"I don't know," Father Murray said. "I really don't know, Lewis. I mean, I understand where you're going, but I'm not sure if we can."

"Even just keep it contained out there. We can keep everyone away from them and try to get back to something similar to normal."

"Normal. Will we ever be normal again? That is the question," Father Murray said.

Lewis sat back from the table and rubbed his brow. "Seems we've had this conversation a few times before. Things returned to normal."

"True, but that was because Edward came home," Father Murray said.

That was enough to uncap the volcano that brewed under the surface inside Jacob. The topic of returning to normal reminded him that no matter how *normal* the town returned, his life would never be normal. They wanted to contain his sister, not help her. And they completely forgot about his father. His father who lay, now alone, in a hospital room. His father, who they credited with returning the town to normal. His father, who no one had talked about how to help. "Come on!" he shouted.

"There has to be something you can do for my father and sister." Both hands hit the table, hard. It was more of a reflex than an intentional move.

It startled all but one, and that one wasn't Jacob. He was just as surprised by it as the other two. Father Lucian, on the other hand, was not, or at least gave no indication he was. He appeared lost in thought and didn't say a word as he stood up and walked around the table and back to the bedroom. He just passed the doorframe when he paused and asked, "Father, do you mind if I make a phone call?"

"Well... of course. No need to ask," Father Murray responded.

His tall and thin frame disappeared through the door, which he pushed slightly closed. While he was out of the room, Father Murray and Lewis resumed their conversation about next steps, much to Jacob's continued disappointment. It was building up in him again and was about to explode when a moment of maturity overcame him, and he pushed up from the table to walk into the kitchen. Just removing himself from the situation helped a little as he stood and stared out the window over the kitchen sink. There wasn't anything he looked at that calmed him. It was night, and outside the window all he saw was a slight shadow where the woods edged the property and then the night sky above them.

Being so far away from any major metropolitan location gave those who lived in Miller's Crossing a perfect view of the night sky. That was something Jacob learned to appreciate. In Portland, they saw the moon and a few stars, but that was it. On their first night in Miller's Crossing, his father took him out into the pasture and told him to look up. There he saw an ocean of stars, more than he ever imagined could exist. Edward had pointed out a few stars that he remembered his father pointing out to him as a child, then others he later learned about as a cub scout. He told Jacob he felt bad for the other scouts. Even on the camping trips, the lights from the nearby cities robbed them of the views he remembered. On that night, after he pointed out the North Star and the Big Dipper, he told Jacob that his own father had told him to look to the stars when you were confused, worried, or stressed. "Look to the heavens for the answers" was the exact phrase he said. Then he explained, there won't be a magical voice that gives you the answer, but if you let your mind wander among the stars and realize how insignificant your problem is compared to the size of the universe, it puts everything into perspective. Jacob remembered giving his father a funny look at that, to which his father responded, "I didn't get it either at your age, but I did later in my life. My father said the same thing when I looked at him like you're looking at me now."

As he looked at the stars visible through the parting clouds, his mind didn't struggle to realize how large the universe was and how small a part of it he was, but that didn't seem to make his problems seem small. In *his universe* they were huge and all-consuming. There would be nothing that would minimize it or make it go away for him. No matter where they set up the roadblocks Lewis was talking about in the other room. No matter who they moved out of danger. The problem still existed. His world was still destroyed. His family was still... gone.

"Jacob."

Jacob spun away from the window and saw Father Murray leaning in through the doorway. "Father Lucian is back. Care to join us?"

Jacob walked back in and retook his seat at the table. Father Lucian sat across from him, back board-straight, face confident. He began when Jacob settled into his chair.

"I have conferred with my superiors. All agree. What is happening here is not just a danger to this location but to the entire world. That is not to be taken as being overdramatic. Remember, this a significantly spiritually active place in the world. An area where the two realms overlap. If a demon were able to get control of it, they could open a portal with little difficulty and let others in. The fact that it has control of your sister, with her knowledge and abilities, is more of a danger. That may have already happened. Left unchecked, evil will spread out from here, endangering others and, what may be the worst fear of my superiors, letting a part of the world we have worked very hard to keep private become very public. The greater world is not ready to realize that the evil they flock to see in movie theaters really exists. We do have an idea, but I need each of you to understand there is no guarantee this will work." He paused and leaned onto the table. His forearms rested flat on the surface, eyes looking right into Jacob's, which made Jacob uncomfortable. "Mr. Meyer... Jacob, I want you to know we will do everything we can for your sister and father, but I can't make you any promises beyond that. Our focus is ending this. Do you understand?"

Jacob swallowed hard to digest what that meant. It was something he wasn't ready to accept, but he didn't see any other option. "Yes, sir," he said wearily.

Lewis reached over and put a hand on his right shoulder.

"As each of you are aware, I am sure, there are six other places in the world like Miller's Crossing. We have assigned each a family to keep it safe. Each of those families have been serving that post for hundreds and in some cases thousands of years. They have seen things I can't even fathom. We are bringing a member of each of those families here to assess the situation and to help."

"When will they arrive?" asked Father Murray.

"Two days. They are each being contacted now and will travel immediately."

9

Jacob spent the next two days where he'd spent the previous six, the hospital room next to his father. Deputy Wendy Tolliver gave him a ride back to his home twice to take a shower and get a fresh change of clothes. That was the first time Jacob had stepped foot back in his home since what happened. It was weird. This was not the first time he came home to an empty house. That was a rather common occurrence. It was knowing that neither his father nor his sister would be coming home later tonight that was different. Knowing that made the entire house feel empty and unfamiliar.

He never turned the television on or anything for any noise. It was just in and out. Wendy's radio echoed updates on the happenings in town through the house. This gave Jacob a more detailed view of what was going on than either Sheriff Tillingsly or Father Murray were telling him. Deputy Tony Yale was spending his day running hourly patrols through town. When not driving through town, he was camped out on State Road 192, watching the single grove of trees in the distance for any activity, which there hadn't been for a few days now. Ted Barton used his spot in the storeroom of his grocery and mercantile store as a lookout and called in updates pretty regularly. Most of the times were just to say nothing had happened or to ask if anything was happening elsewhere since it was so quiet in town. Others were as well. That seemed to be an overwhelming theme to the radio traffic. Nothing was going on, and people were getting nervous. Jacob shared that feeling.

Back in the hospital, all was quiet, but unlike the world outside those walls where quiet was a good thing, Jacob would give anything for something to happen inside. Anything would be better than nothing. Visitors stopped by often. Father Murray had left his normal perch to assist Father Lucian in preparing for their visitors. His home was far too small to accommodate seven more people, so he reached out to members of his parish and arranged housing. Many were close friends of the Meyer family and offered to do anything they could to help. Charlotte Stance took in two, as did her family. Mark Grier offered to take one in, along with Jacob. He had attempted to get Jacob to come stay with him and his wife instead of spending every day and night at the hospital. His son's old room was still set up and available. Jacob had considered it but so far refused. It was an offer he might break down and accept soon , though. The last two would be the houseguests of Lewis Tillingsly.

When Jacob heard they would fly in, he imagined they would be picked up and brought in on a chartered aircraft, but by the middle of the second day, it was clear that was not the case. Each was flying in on separate commercial flights. Each required multiple connections before arriving at Dulles International, just about an hour away. Their arrival times were split all throughout the day. Jacob overheard that those who volunteered to let one of the arriving guests stay with them were leaving around eleven a.m. that morning to go meet them all at the airport. He didn't know for sure what time they got back, he could only assume it was late since Father Murray stopped by the hospital at just after nine to check on him and Edward.

The question was the same as it always was. "Any change?"

Jacob's response was the same too, and almost robotic. "No. No movement."

Father Murray walked toward the head of Edward's bed, crossed him, and said a prayer like he had every night.

"Jacob, we are all getting together at the church in the morning. I'll pick you up. Why not come home with me, or let me drop you off at the Griers, so you can get a good night's sleep?"

"Nah. I'm good here," Jacob responded.

"You sure?"

"Yes, sir."

"All right. I will be here around eight," Father Murray said as he turned to walk out of the room. On his way out, he patted the red recliner he had spent the better part of the last week in. "You should try this one. It's more comfortable."

Jacob didn't respond, but his mind considered it. His body waited to react until the father had left. The cushions molded around his body as he sat down. A shift of his weight backward reclined the chair to almost flat. His back appreciated the comfort of the chair, as did his neck, shoulders, and hips. It wasn't long before the darkness in his mind matched the darkness outside the room. He hadn't felt tired before he sat in the chair. The momentary comfort that came over his body allowed his consciousness to seek a similar comfort. His breathing slowed, and he was out.

The calm of his sleeping state didn't last. Jacob's mind wandered in and out of various topics and images. Each involved his father and sister. Each carried a feeling of loss and pain with them. He called out several times for Sarah. Still unsure if what he had experienced twice before was real or a dream, his subconscious still tried. There was no answer. Just the images and darkness. When he gave up, a part of him accepted that when all this was over, he would just be left with images and darkness, nothing else. The family he once had would be no more. His soul felt alone.

The feeling was enough to stick with him when he shook awake, just after four in the morning. His eyes caught a nurse leaving the room as he sat up, and he could only assume she bumped the chair while tending to his father. The chair was close to the bed. Something he remediated with a few scoots backward and a twist to put it parallel against the wall. That created a wide space for anyone who needed to tend to his father.

Jacob leaned it back again, hoping to slip back into sleep. Instead, the feeling that lingered played deeper in his mind while he was awake. It wasn't pictures of his father or sister this time. It was thoughts about the future. His future. Could he still live here? That was the question his mind didn't have a problem answering. Too many memories were a big part of that answer. The larger part was about the people he would have to face daily. The people his family hurt and devastated. Where would he go?

Jacob rolled on his side. The new position didn't chase the thought away. Nor did it invite in sleep. He got up and walked out into the quiet hall. They dimmed the lights so only every third light was on. He followed the alternating pools of light and darkness down the hallway to the sunroom, which was not lit up by the sun at the moment. The lights were all off, bathing it in darkness. From there he had a good view of the night sky, with their town of Miller's Crossing below. The town he would need to leave.

That was his last thought until he heard, "Jacob. Jacob. Time to wake up."

Jacob opened his eyes and looked up at Father Murray. At some point after he sat down on the ratty sofa in the sunroom, his body and mind finally both agreed, and he slipped away. He had no intention of falling asleep down there. It was just a change of scenery to clear his mind. It had obviously worked. Or so he hoped.

"What time is it?"

"Half past seven."

A big stretch preceded, "Give me just a few, and I'll be ready." Jacob felt surprisingly refreshed. The sofa looked like it would be hard and lumpy, with springs sticking you through what was left of the cushions, but it was rather comfortable. Something he would have to remember for tonight and the rest of the time he stayed up here.

"You got time."

Jacob didn't need a lot of time. He was more expedient than his sister at getting ready. Instead of the several-hour routine she went through, he just threw a splash or two of water in his face and ran his fingers through his hair. Before he left the bathroom in his father's room, he brushed his teeth, a must, and then threw on a fresh change of clothes. Jeans, plain white T-shirt, and his school hoodie. A constant wardrobe choice between the months of September and March, when there was enough chill in the air to need sleeves.

Jacob rode with Father Murray over to the church mostly in silence. Being one of the few times Jacob had seen these areas of Miller's Crossing during the day since, he was astonished by how much it had changed. The normally busy sidewalks in the center of town were empty. Shop after shop showed every sign of being not just closed but boarded up. The wind had piled up leaves and small bits of debris against sides of buildings and in the gutters. Something the city refuse department would never let happen under normal circumstances. They cleared the streets and sidewalks by dawn, every day.

Weeds were visible above the carpet of leaves in front of the high school. The small baseball diamond next to the elementary school was just a patch of dry clay. No white lines, which were always visible from the twice-a-week games and practices held there. An orange cloud of dust rose up from it as the wind crossed it. No one had tended to it by watering it down.

The sign on the elementary school advertised the upcoming "Fal_ Festi_al." The second F hung on for its life to the bottom rail of the sign against the breeze. Jacob knew what it was. It was the highlight of his years at that school, and a must-attend for everyone else in town regardless if you had a child of school age or not. The date was next Saturday. At the moment, chances seemed bleak for that happening.

The lack of cars on the road was obvious. Not that there was a traffic problem in Miller's Crossing, but you always passed a few cars on the road everywhere you went. Being the only car sitting at a traffic signal at this time of morning was a rare occurrence. Not seeing another car anywhere, up and down both of the roads Jacob could see, was beyond rare. The only thing keeping the scene from classifying as desolate was the lack of tumbleweeds blowing down the pavement. The leaves dancing in a whirlwind would have to do.

They pulled into the church's gravel-covered parking lot. Several cars were already there, but no one was outside. Jacob assumed everyone was already inside waiting on them. He looked at his phone. They weren't late. The others were possibly just early.

Father Murray brought the car to a stop and opened the driver's side door. He placed one foot on the gravel when Jacob opened the passenger side door with a squeak that sent several birds fleeing from a nearby oak and its colorful red and orange foliage. They climbed rapidly away from the noise, which had ceased, leaving just the sound of their own wings against the air and their bodies.

"Jacob," Father Murray called.

Jacob stopped with one foot already out of the car and turned back toward the father.

"Two things."

"Yes, Father," Jacob said with a hint of question in his voice.

"These visitors are going to ask you a lot of questions. Father Lucian said the more they know about you, your father, and Sarah, the better. Just answer them. Hide nothing. There is no reason to. Think of these people as family. You all share a similar responsibility and bond."

"Yes, sir," Jacob said. The thought of playing twenty questions with people he didn't know was not appealing. It was a game he had been playing himself twenty-four hours a day.

"Second... and I'm not sure how to explain this. Try not to stare. Some of them are... well, not used to being around people and are a little... different."

Jacob followed Father Murray up to the church. He stopped after his first step up the front stairs and let his head roam to his right to take in what he saw out of the corner of his eye. Off to the side of the church, nestled back among the trees, was a single round structure. It resembled a tent, but not one covered by the typical vinyl or canvas he was familiar with. It was something more rustic, more raw. Smoke still rose above the remnants of a fire pit constructed just in front of the doorway.

10

Jacob had walked into the church several hundred times since returning to Miller's Crossing. On top of every Sunday and holiday, this was a regular place for his family to visit to sit and talk with Father Murray. Waiting on their father as *he* talked to Father Murray was more like it. Sarah had had conversations, more so after she returned from the Vatican. Jacob never had more than a handful. Mostly just attempts by a family friend to reach out to the younger generation and talk. It fascinated him how much the father knew about sports, something that didn't fit his impression of a priest.

Walking in this time was different. Completely different. He stepped into a whole other world, in the confines of something familiar. He wasn't the only one. Mark Grier and Lewis Tillingsly stood in the back, just inside the door. Both were taking in the scene of the guests assembled at the front. Jacob paused by them and let Father Murray go ahead up to the front. Father Lucian warmly greeted him and then made introductions.

"Is that them?" Jacob asked.

"Yeeep," Mark Grier said.

"What are they like?" he asked, his eyes going over them one by one. Taking in their appearance. Their dress. How they stood and moved.

"Well... it might not be polite to say, but odd," Mark said. "See that guy in the black waistcoat with brass buttons?"

"Yes."

"He's staying with me, along with the woman there in the long dress. The guy slept standing up, all night long."

Jacob looked at Mark as if he was pulling his leg. "You're just messing with me."

"No lie." His right hand sprang up like he was taking an oath. "When I went to wake him this morning, he was asleep, standing, in the dark, pressed into the corner."

"Trade ya," Lewis said. "That chap there in the Doctor Dolittle hat, a Mr. Lionel James Halensworth. When we got home, he asked if I would like to share a drink. I obliged. Then had another, and then another. Each round began with a challenge aimed at me and the one in the bow tie, Mr. Nagoti, to a drinking contest. I haven't felt this hungover since I was," he paused and looked at Jacob, "your age. Mind you, times were different back then. You need to wait until you're older."

"Jacob," Father Murray called. "Come on up here. We have some people you need to meet."

His beckon silenced the hum of several individual conversations and caused every eye in the building to focus on him. Jacob took one step, and then a second. The second step was followed by another one that lacked confidence, but he proceeded in putting enough steps together to reach the gathered mass up front, and he only looked back at the two familiar faces at the back half a dozen times.

At the front, several walked forward with their hands extended toward Jacob. Their movement overwhelmed him and sent him a step backward. That prompted a similar response for those who approached him. But only in their movements. Their facial expressions hadn't changed. His reaction didn't shock or surprise them. Neither were their expressions warm and welcoming. To Jacob, they looked curious. That was the word he felt best described how they looked at him. They looked at him with the curiosity of a medical student studying a lab rat for his reaction when exposed to a new maze, smell, or drug.

"Jacob, I would like for you to meet Madame Catherine Stryvia, from Bulgaria. Her family takes care of the Rila Lakes." The woman, a raven-haired beauty in her mid-thirties, looked like something straight out of a gothic horror movie. Pale white complexion, long black dress, and a red cape completed the look.

She extended her hand again. This time Jacob took it. Her grip was firm but dainty at the same time. The curious look she had on her face a few moments ago hadn't changed. She studied him. Again he felt like that lab rat.

"I had the honor of meeting your sister at the Vatican," she said. Her accent was thick, and her tone cut through the air, but there was a hint of warmth and compassion in it.

The man in the bow tie, Mr. Nagoti from Japan, was the next introduced. He said nothing. Just shook Jacob's hand and bowed slightly. Jacob wasn't sure if he should do the same at first. He started, then stopped, and then finished it rather awkwardly. The man's stony expression cracked ever so slightly.

Jacob had barely released Mr. Nagoti's hand when two beefy hands grabbed and yanked him in for a tight and uncomfortable embrace against the girth of the man in the Doolittle hat. "How you doing there, Jacob?" said the voice of Mr. Halensworth. The embrace had plastered Jacob's ear against the man's chest such that he could hear it echo inside his frame. The aromatic scents of the drink, or drinks, of choice from the night before were still present with every word.

"I'm okay," he croaked. Which was all he could do.

"Chin up, lad. We're here."

Next up, behind Mr. Halensworth, stood a small-framed man. Bald, with a pleasant smile. He moved forward briskly and took Jacob's hand.

Father Murray handled the introductions. "Jacob, this is Tenzein Mao, a monk from Tibet." The man shook his head up and down when he heard his own name. "He is the most experienced in the room, besides Father Lucian, that is. Mao took over for his father when he was a few years younger than you. He is now eighty-three."

Jacob hoped he didn't act as surprised on the outside as he was on the inside. There was no way the man in front of him was any older than forty. Not a wrinkle on the man's face, not even a smile line. Not from a lack of smiling either. He had that kind of face that looked like it was always smiling and pleasant. A man who always looked to the brighter side of life.

"This is Lord Marcus Negiev, from Lithuania."

The man who reached forward for Jacob's hand with both of his was the one in the black waistcoat and brass buttons that Mark Grier had pointed out. Jacob thought his father's friend was pulling his leg with the story of the man sleeping standing up in a dark corner. Now, face-to-face with the mysterious man, he believed every word. His features were pale and gaunt under a mob of jet-black hair combed straight down on all sides. Eyes sunken in, but not lost for life. They examined Jacob and the rest of the assembled visitors.

"It is good to meet you, Mr. Meyer," he said, without the lisp that Jacob had expected.

"It is good to meet you too," was all he could muster, while his mind repeated over and over Father Murray's earlier warning. *Don't stare. Don't stare.* Easier said than done, as the man standing before him probed Jacob's essence with his eyes.

Jacob pulled his hand away from the man's clammy two-handed shake. He then moved out of their way. There was no one left to meet, or so Jacob thought. He now stood at the front of the church, through the mass of people who stood around the first two pews. Father Murray made several nods to Jacob's right. Neither of which Jacob understood and looked at him curiously. The next motion, the point of a finger, was a clearer signal. Jacob followed the direction of the finger to see a single person sitting at the end of the first pew. The mass of people had previously blocked his view of her presence. The person, a woman covered in what appeared to be furs, looked uncomfortable and out of place, pressed as far to the other end of the pew as she could get. Her head and face hid behind a mass of wild hair, gaze locked on the floor. Her body swayed ever so slightly forward and back.

Jacob started her way, but Father Murray grabbed his arm. "We can meet her later. She is from a tiny village in Brazil that she has never left before. She is not that comfortable around people. Best to just leave her be for now."

"Is she..." Jacob paused and pointed in the direction of the tent and fire he spotted outside.

"Yep, that's where she slept. She brought her own tent. Wasn't comfortable inside the house."

11

"Thank you all for coming," announced Father Lucian. The normally calm and quiet priest raised his voice to break up a few of the conversations still going on among the group. "Let's take a seat," he said, again louder than he normally spoke.

A few of the party were being stubborn, but they now heeded his call as silence descended over the sanctum.

"Jacob, you come up here with me."

Jacob joined Father Lucian, a man he towered over by almost half a foot. This added to his feeling that he was on display. It didn't help that every set of eyes in the room watched his every move.

"Again, thank you all for coming such a long way. There is not much more I can tell you than I did over the phone. One of our own keepers has been possessed and put this town under siege. She may have been possessed by the demon even at the time we were training her."

A murmur once again broke the silence as each of the people sitting in the pews turned to comment to the person next to them. Each had lost the look of curiosity they had earlier and now shared one of concern.

"I know. I know. I am not sure if that is the case, but I do know what it means if it were true. I believe we need to proceed believing that whatever has her knows everything we do. She may be strong enough to resist and guard our secrets, but we won't know."

"Father," Mr. Negiev said as he stood up. He tugged at the bottom of his waistcoat before speaking. "If it is true, and it knows everything we do, what can we do?"

Jacob's despair that had been deepening by the day dropped to a depth he didn't believe it could. It made him realize there was no bottom to that pit.

Father Lucian replied, "It would know what we are taught, but not our experiences. That is why I called each of you. We share a similar background, but that is where it stops. Each of us has a wealth of experience from our own lives and what our ancestors handed down to us. It is that which we need."

Everyone seated seemed satisfied by the answer. They nodded at one another.

"Here is what I can tell you from what I have been told and seen for myself," Father Lucian continued. "She is out there trapped by a creature that either has opened or is trying to open the portal. There are several creatures as well as some animals with it under its control. From what I can tell, those beings have been here for a while, so they haven't come through recently, which is why I am not sure if it has opened a portal yet. I have been told they stay in that shed most of the time but have come out and roamed through the town at least once."

Father Murray held up three fingers from his seat in the front pew.

"Three times before. Each time, they sought out and attacked anyone they encountered," Father Lucian said. The last statement sounded like more of a question, each word said with a slight pause between it and the next as Father Murray confirmed the statement with a nod, one word at a time. "It is not scared of us. When I went out there, it actively probed my thoughts to see if it could get in. It wants to control." He paused and took a breath that was long and deep. Jacob could hear the air moving through the man from where he stood next to him. "I believe it is Abaddon."

"Psh," said Mr. Halensworth, his lips upturned and puckered. "We have all dealt with one of his minions before. I have lost count."

Mr. Negiev and Madame Stryvia both laughed. She turned her head away from her counterpart from the United Kingdom. Mr. Negiev snipped back, "I seriously doubt that, my friend. If you have, I could count the text messages you sent me every time you've dealt with anything."

"Yeah, yeah. You owe me a few drinks for some of those," dismissed Mr. Halensworth. The shot didn't appear to harm his pride any. "Father, what makes this one so dangerous? We have all done battle with one of those before."

"Because this time, it is him," Father Lucian said frankly.

The jovial banter that preceded this announcement stopped, and for the first time since he entered the church, Jacob believed the others in the room looked how he felt.

"You mean, the actual demon?" Mao asked.

"Yes, he was released several decades ago and not put back in."

"And we were not told?" stammered Madame Stryvia.

For the next fifteen minutes, Father Lucian recapped the details of how Abaddon was released by Father Murray years ago. The story caused several disapproving looks in Father Murray's direction. Each of which appeared to make him uncomfortable.

Nothing appeared to bother him more so than the eruption by Lord Negiev. "A keeper's post was abandoned? There are rules about this. Why was it not reported? Why was another not placed?" Each question directed at Father Murray. Each question delivered harshly. Each question left there in the air with no definitive answer.

Father Lucian did his best to dismiss it, but the realization caused a stir.

Jacob stood there and listened to the story. Some of which he had heard, but much he hadn't. His father had only told him his grandparents had died. It was something they talked about when he was younger. Jacob couldn't remember why anymore. Probably some random question his four- or five-year-old self asked. It came up again when they returned to the family farm. Each time he was told, he was too young for his mind to consider any reason for someone to die other than illness or old age. Since then, it had never come up. His gaze wandered, as did those of the rest of the room when they figured out Father Murray was responsible for their deaths. This added to the darkness that had hung over Jacob for the past nine days. What it added wasn't more despair and loss, it was fear.

"We should not dwell on the past. Our focus needs to be on why we are here," Father Lucian explained in an attempt to calm and refocus the group. It worked. The room was instantly silent. "We need to perform an exorcism, one I believe will take our combined skills and experiences. This won't be easy. There should be no illusions of that. I must be truthful. I'm not even sure it is possible, but we must try. This concerns all of us. If this town is lost, it poses a threat to each of yours, and everywhere else too."

"Father." Lord Negiev stood up. "We need to know, does it have the relic?"

Father Lucian turned to Jacob. The attention of the room followed. His hand reached inside his right pants pocket. It felt the object. The one that was so familiar to his father but so foreign to him. Just two pieces of wood put together in a shape. Out he pulled it, and when the first bit of wood breached the top of his pocket, there was a collective sigh in the room. With it fully out, he placed it flat on his hand and offered it to Father Lucian. The old priest reached over but didn't take the object. Instead he closed Jacob's fingers around it.

"Jacob, have you?" asked Madame Stryvia.

The precise "what" was not asked, but Jacob had an idea what she meant and answered. He knew the twenty questions would start at some point. This was probably it. "My father hasn't trained me or involved me in this side of his life, but I do feel and see ghosts. I have for the past several years."

"So, you have never felt the cross?"

"No. Not in the way I think you mean. I have held it and read through the book, but that was it."

"But you know about it? Have seen it used, correct?" asked Mr. Halensworth. His body leaned forward while his right hand rubbed his chin.

The answer was clear in his mind. The first and only time had occurred just a few weeks ago outside the homecoming dance. Before that, he had heard about it from both his father and Sarah but had never seen it. "Yes, just a few weeks back. I saw my father use it against a group of demons at our homecoming dance. That was the one and only time."

"And your sister? Ever see her use it?"

"No," Jacob said, but before he finished the answer, something flashed in his mind. It only took another second for him to make sense of its importance. "I never saw her use it, but I do know she didn't always take it."

"What do you mean? She doesn't need a relic?" Madame Stryvia asked, a question that seemed to surprise many of the group. They all leaned forward and mouths fell open. Some covered them with a hand, but others didn't. Leaving them gaping open below raised eyebrows.

"It is true," interjected Father Lucian. "Sarah does not always need the relic. Many times during training, she showed the ability to deal with spirits and even demons without the relic. I took her to observe the exorcism of an eleven-year-old boy, as a purely educational endeavor. I instructed her to just stand off to the side and not say a word. She did exactly as I asked until both me and the attending priest were thrown against the wall. She stepped forward and spoke to the boy. Before we were on our feet, she had dismissed the demon. The boy sat resting comfortably in the chair, alone. When we returned to her apartment, I noticed the cross still sitting on the nightstand."

"Not possible!" exclaimed Lord Negiev.

"Actually, it is." Mr. Nagoti spoke for the first time. He was the only one to this point who hadn't responded or reacted to anything he had heard. He sat straight and unemotional the whole time, which stuck out to Jacob amongst the reactions of everyone else. The only other person who hadn't reacted at all was the one who sat at the end of the pew away from everyone. The dignified man from Japan adjusted his bow tie and continued, "In my culture, there are stories of those in past generations who showed such abilities. It was said they tapped into dark energy and entities to aid them. I believe they partnered with some of the very beings they fought against to use their abilities to help them."

"There are examples of that in all your pasts. Some good, and some bad," Father Lucian said. Jacob fought the urge to look at Father Murray after what he had learned a few minutes ago. "I now believe that explains some of Sarah's capabilities."

"Sheriff? Sheriff? You there?" asked a voice over the radio fastened to the hip of Lewis Tillingsly, standing in the back. The sound forced six heads to twist around, like a cell phone call in a quiet theater. Much like the people who receive those calls, Lewis walked back toward the door to answer. To his disadvantage, they'd designed the church to amplify sound no matter where you were.

"What is it, Tony?"

"They're back. Just getting to town center."

"How many?" Lewis asked.

"Seven. No sign of Sarah though."

With that Mr. Halensworth stood up and declared, "What are we waiting on? Let's go." He scooted past the others and headed toward the back. "Sheriff, please lead the way."

The others were now behind him, as Lewis looked past them and up to the front.

Father Lucian nodded and joined them. "Come on, Jacob."

They stepped outside into a world that reminded Jacob of a horror film. The cool sunny morning that had existed when he entered was gone. Replaced by layer after layer of black clouds, wind that screamed as it passed by, and rolling thunder with every eye-blinding flash of lightning. He didn't remember rain being in the forecast for the day or any weather alerts on his phone.

"It knows we are here. I felt it as soon as I arrived," said the final, and eremite, member of their party with a hiss. A quick tug at the fur she wore pulled it tighter around her shoulders before she strolled off toward her tent in the woods.

12

Jacob was in the second of four cars that sped through the backroads of Miller's Crossing. Sheriff Lewis Tillingsly drove the lead car, but there were no lights or sirens. It was his personal Plymouth, not a cruiser with the light bar. That didn't stop them from blowing through several traffic signals on the way. No other cars were out on the road. The only factor that made it dangerous was how dark it had gotten. It was a little before ten in the morning, but it was already as dark as ten at night. Streetlights were on, and their headlights led the way. Dark trees lined the route, trees they only saw during the brief and blinding strikes of lightning that seemed to follow them from the church along their trek.

In the car with Jacob and Father Murray were Tenzein Mao and the mystery lady whose name Jacob had yet to hear. Both sat in the back behind them and were praying to themselves silently or in their own native language.

"Young Meyer, you have seen demons only once, yes?" asked Tenzein after he completed his prayer.

"Twice," Jacob answered.

"Oh, so not just with your father?" he asked.

"I snuck out a few nights ago and saw them," Jacob responded, and then added, "and my sister."

"You saw your sister?"

"Yes, sir."

"Did she see you?"

"No." Then Jacob remembered his dream and corrected himself. "Yes. Maybe. I'm not sure."

"This is a confusing time for you, I am sure. Lots of emotions rolling around in you," Tenzein said. He leaned forward against the back of the front seat. "Emotions are strong energy, but you have to control them. Uncontrolled, they will betray you. The secret is you need to have a calm mind. Can you do that?"

Calm was not the word Jacob would use to describe his emotional state at the moment. At best, he was a hurricane that was still gaining strength, and he ricocheted between anger, depression, despair, hopelessness, and back again, over and over, every minute of every day.

"Probably not," the monk answered his own question. "Do this. Imagine the calmest body of water you have ever seen. The glassy surface of a clear lake. No waves, no wake. Then imagine yourself floating on it. Only your face is above the water. The water filters everything from the universe around you, leaving you with the serene peace of nothingness. The water has done its job, now you have to do yours. Ignore everything you are feeling, everything you are thinking. Focus on one purpose. No ripples in the water. You disturb the water, you disturb the balance of the universe and invite chaos. You no disturb the water, you are in control of the universe."

Jacob's mind wandered through the scene Tenzein described. He remembered the feeling of swimming and lying in the tub with his head submerged but his face still above the water. Every sound around him—the screaming and yelling of the other kids at the community pool, the music his mom played during his bath time—all of it muted. It was there, but he was in a peaceful place. A world he could easily become lost in. The rest of it he had his doubts about. His body and mind felt jittery and unfocused. "Does it work?" he asked.

"Yes. I meditate using that image twice a day, every day. I also do it before I confront anything. I didn't always. I was a few years younger than your age when my father died and left me this responsibility. A village two mountains away sent for me, and I rushed in, unfocused." Tenzein stopped and, with his right hand, rolled up the sleeve on his left arm. A large scar stretched from his wrist up past his elbow. It was jagged, not clean and surgical. Obvious gaps in the muscle under the skin created craters. "I was foolish and paid the price. I sought wisdom from my elders. They turned me to the teachings of our religion beyond those about the spiritual world that they taught me. My religion taught me to center my mind, body, and soul. Through that wisdom, I have been able to overcome all challenges. It tells me we will overcome the danger we both feel now."

He was right. Jacob felt it. He had for the last few minutes. It started as just an icy chill but progressed to a shiver that traveled up and down his body. Pins pricked the surface of his gooseflesh skin. The shops and buildings in the center of town were visible far ahead of them. No signs of anything else. At least visually. They were there. No question about that.

Lewis pulled off to the side of the road about a quarter of a mile before the buildings. The rest of the cars pulled in behind him. It wasn't long before their occupants all stood outside the cars, all facing the buildings.

"They're there. That is for sure," announced Mr. Halensworth.

They all knew it and nodded. There was something else too. Jacob felt it but wasn't sure if anyone else did. He was being watched. Not by anything close, but by something far away. Its attention was on him and him alone.

13

Lord Negiev and Mr. Halensworth took the lead. Neither appeared to take the danger too seriously. Each took turns and called out whatever was there.

"Come on. Where are you?" Mr. Halensworth bellowed.

"Are you hiding from us?" Lord Negiev asked. His tone taunted the air.

The rest followed several feet behind them. Each acted as if they took their surroundings with a level of reverence the other two had forgotten.

"Come on. I wanted to see how big and bad you are," the brash Englishman bellowed.

Jacob heard Madame Stryvia retort, "Idiots" just under her breath. It was easy for him to hear her, even as quietly as she said it. There wasn't a sound coming from anywhere. No crickets. No wind. Even the thunder had subsided. In the horror movies he enjoyed, the lead character would say, "It's quiet, too quiet," and eerie music would play in the background to foreshadow the impending arrival of whatever evil the story was about. He now found himself in that same setting, except without the eerie music. It wasn't needed. The stillness combined with the cold chill and the feeling of being watched was more than enough to give Jacob the biggest case of the creeps he had ever felt and put his head on a turnstile. Left, then right. Nothing. Even behind him, nothing around them except darkness and an empty street he had been on hundreds of times before, but never like this. It was mid-morning but appeared to be the middle of the night.

Up ahead of him, Mr. Halensworth had stopped and taken off his brown sport coat, folded it up and placed it neatly on one of the several park benches that lined the shopping district. On a normal day, with the sun out like this day started with, it would be uncommon to find these benches empty. People would stop to sit and talk, and others made special trips with their morning coffee to sit there and read the paper while greeting everyone who walked by. The Doctor Dolittle hat joined them on the bench. Then, he pushed both sleeves of his starched, white button-up shirt to his elbow, displaying the forearms of a man who had been in a few fights throughout the years.

His compatriot at the front removed nothing but did spread out slightly toward the other side of the road. A quick tug of his waistcoat and a pop of his neck to the right preceded the plunging of his hand into his right pants pocket. It came out as quickly as it went in. With it, a long string and a cross that looked oddly familiar to Jacob. An instinctual glance down at the one still in his right hand confirmed it.

"In case you are wondering Jacob, they all have one. We divided the original crucifix up into crosses for each site. Yours being the last," explained Father Murray from just behind Jacob. "The assignment of a keeper used to be reserved for a member of the clergy, a priest, but your family broke that tradition. Since then, assignment followed ability."

Mr. Halensworth had his out in his hand as well and was now whistling, as if calling a dog.

"So childish," Madame Stryvia mumbled under her breath, just in front of Jacob. Her pace quickened, quickly leaving the others behind, and she joined the two she just admonished. Her red cape fell to the ground with a flourish, revealing the cross hung around her neck.

"Don't antagonize them, you fools," she admonished them again. "Can't you feel their angst?"

"Of course I can. We all can. I just don't like not being able to see them," answered Halensworth, his voice less brazen than before. "I would rather they come on out than this stupid cat-and-mouse game."

"That I agree with," she said.

"Same," agreed Lord Negiev.

The three walked further ahead of the rest and then all stopped, midstride, on the same step.

"Which side?" Madame Stryvia asked, her gaze locked straight down the road.

A chorus of "left" and "right" answers emerged from the assembled keepers. All except Jacob, that was. He was late with his answer. He felt it, and he knew what he felt. There was no way he could miss it. It started as a soft chill on one side, then the other. Then it built, fast, and rampaged through his essence with the ferocity of a speeding freight train until it exploded out. "BOTH!"

Jacob's voice pierced the silence of the night just as two large creatures jumped from the roofs of the buildings on either side of the road. They landed mere feet in front of the trio that took the lead. None backed up and gave any ground. Instead they adjusted their stance and held the ground. The creatures, a combination of human and animal that nightmares were made of, both stood at least ten feet tall and snorted and snarled.

"Watch it, they are not alone!" exclaimed Mr. Nagoti.

"Where at?" Lord Negiev asked. His hand shot forward. The cross dangled in front of him toward the beasts. They recoiled against its presence but didn't flee, didn't retreat.

He didn't have to wait long before they answered his question. Two more leaped in from the same buildings, and another emerged from a side street. All three strolled forward. No urgency in their unnatural gait. Snorts and snarls accompanied their breathing. Puffs of smoke emanated from their nostrils. Two pairs of clawed hands dragged against the pavement, producing sparks. Another claw dragged against the glass of a storefront window. It made the sound of fingernails on a chalkboard sound like the sweetest aria. The glass above the line created by the claw fell from the window frame and shattered on the sidewalk. They left trails of flame behind every step. This was something Jacob hadn't seen that night at the high school, nor when he snuck out. It drove a fear deep inside of him. One thought jumped into his mind, *This is Old Testament fire and brimstone stuff.*

A crumpled metal trash can crashed and slid to a stop on the pavement in front of him. The creature that had thrown it stood and screamed in a hundred voices while it watched the can fly through the air.

"Mark, Lewis, you might want to go get behind the cars," warned Father Murray.

"No objection, Father," responded Lewis. He was already several steps away, and Mark had already reached the bumper before the father had completed his suggestion.

"Is that all of them?" Mr. Halensworth asked.

"I think so, but not sure," responded Madame Stryvia. "There is such an evil feel to this place. I can't tell if there is anything else."

"I know," he replied. "So, guys, what do you say about returning to your area of the woods and we all get together to do this later? No need for you to get hurt now."

The offer to walk away was refused, as one creature swiped at Lord Negiev. He dodged and rolled to the ground.

"That would be a no," Mr. Halensworth said with a grunt as he charged the beast directly in front of him. A wild swing of his cross missed. "Foul creature, you do not belong in our Lord's world..." he began. The longer he spoke, the brighter the light that resonated from the cross.

Lord Negiev was now back to his feet and made his own swipe at his foe but missed as well. The creature returned the favor and connected. The impact sent him rolling back on the road. He jumped up and slapped at the spot on his waistcoat where it made contact. It smoldered with small black flames emanating out from the center. The slaps did nothing to extinguish the flames, only producing sparks with every whack. Quickly, he threw off the coat, leaving it in a smoking pile on the road. Then, after he adjusted his red velvet vest, he marched forward and declared, "This one is mine."

His counterpart couldn't hear him, he was too busy sliding on the asphalt after another thunderous strike sent him flying to the ground. The sound of it echoed around them and rumbled the ground they stood on.

"Let's not let them have all the fun," said Mr. Nagoti. He, Father Lucian, and Tenzein Mao moved forward. Each pulled out their own crosses.

Tenzein Mao looked back at Jacob and said, "Remember, Jacob, peaceful mind. Imagine the water."

The last member of their party followed the others forward but remained a few steps behind. She observed everything around her carefully, cautiously. Jacob did the same. The sensations overwhelmed him. He could no longer feel a single entity or even the five he saw. There was an overbearing evil. Both in his mind and in his physical being. Acid crept up his throat, and his legs shook but stayed locked to the ground. Several attempts to step forward resulted in a buckle in his knees that he caught before anyone else noticed. A voice in the back of his head reminded him this was his town, and his family caused this. The voice nagged him and ate away at what was not consumed by fear and that feeling of evil all around him. It was down to its last bite when he gave himself the talk. It wasn't a pep talk or an inspiration speech. Nothing the climactic scene of a movie could be made from. It was guilt. The guilt he felt as he watched several strangers now sprawled across the roadway as they attempted to confront the demons in his town. The demons his sister, possessed or not, let out and sent into town to confront them.

One wailed in the depths of his consciousness as Mr. Halensworth made firm contact with the cross and sent it back where it came from. "That's one," he exclaimed. "How many for you, Negiev?"

Jacob stepped forward. One step. Really it was less than a step, more of a half of a step, which was all he could muster under the weight of everything he felt and what was in his mind. Father Murray voiced a warning, "Jacob..." from behind him, but a supernatural event interrupted the rest of the message. A single bright white lightning bolt shot from the sky and struck a spot about an inch in front of Jacob's right foot. The foot that had taken the step. An explosion rocketed through the air with the blinding light, stopping both keepers and creatures in their place. Both Mr. Nagoti and Tenzein Mao took advantage of the distraction. Light shot from both of their crosses and froze two of the creatures in their tracks. They dismissed both quickly in a flash of blue flame and smoke.

The rest weren't having as easy of a time. Lord Negiev chased his target down the road. It fled from him, not on the road itself but along the front of the shops. Its claws crashed into the bricks on the front of the buildings with each step, sending piles of debris raining down.

Madame Stryvia had avoided any contact but had failed to trap or dismiss the one she had targeted. With each attempt she made, it swung at her or moved, forcing her to stop and get out of the way. She yelled, "Enough!" and a flash of light shot from her cross, sending the creature crashing to the ground. It stayed there until it disappeared in a flicker of blue flame and smoke, after she finished the rite of dismissal.

That left two. Both were trying to get away. They could let them and deal with them again, out there, or end it now. A decision that would be made for them, when a tandem wheel pickup, Ted Barton's truck, flew at them from the darkness. A parting gift from one beast, or was it? As the mangled truck bounced past and over them, its friend charged them. Jacob watched, helplessly, as the scene unfolded before him. All were on the ground, where they landed to avoid the truck. None would have time to get up to avoid the approaching creatures who, along with Jacob's pulse, were picking up the pace at an astonishing rate. Their steps, and every beat of his heart, echoed in his head like explosions.

A scream, a primal scream, unlike anything Jacob had ever heard, rocketed through the air with a flash of light. The sound and light knocked both creatures to the ground, where they wailed in pain. The scream came from the silent member of their group. The one who had yet to be introduced. She knelt on the ground and watched the others finish the creatures off before she got up and walked away into the darkness.

14

"Everyone all right?" Father Murray asked.

"No worse for wear," Halensworth said. He examined the scrapes on his arms and then rubbed the trickle of blood coming down his forehead, which he hit on the ground while avoiding a wild swing. "Well, maybe a little wear."

"I'm okay," Lord Negiev said.

Madame Stryvia helped him to his feet. Jacob saw scrapes on him as well, but what really got his attention was the mark that was still smoldering on his shirtsleeve. There were no visible flames, but there was smoke. Smoke that slowly rose from the spot and lingered just above him for an unnatural amount of time. His jacket still sat in a pile on the ground and smoldered with the same unsettling smoke. Both Madame Stryvia and Lord Negiev attempted to smother the spot, but it continued to smoke. Neither appeared to suffer any burns from the contact.

Jacob walked over to the piled-up waistcoat on the ground. He ran his hand over it and through the smoke. There was no heat. This was not like any fire he had ever experienced. It was cool and icy the closer he moved his hand to it. The texture and tone of his skin changed the longer he left it in the smoke. It took on a gray shriveled-up appearance while in the smoke, and normal peach skin returned after it passed through to the other side.

"Let me help you with that," Father Murray said. With a vial he retrieved from his pocket, he walked over.

"Ah yes," remarked Lord Negiev as Father Murray flipped the top of the vial up and dripped a single drop on his sleeve, and then another small drop on his coat. Both stopped smoldering in an instant.

As the keepers regrouped, more scrapes and bruises were evident. Some from impacts with the ground. Others from punches and swipes by the creatures. Luckily none suffered any gashes from the large claws.

"That was a test," Mr. Nagoti stated. "They gave up too easy."

"Agree. It wanted to see who was here. It can undoubtedly feel us, just like we can feel it," said Father Lucian. "Next time won't be so easy."

Everyone seemed to agree, which explained the lack of any collective exhale of relief. They knew this was just the beginning, and it would only get worst. Jacob knew it, too, but what was worse than this? His mind couldn't make that leap. Things had already passed what Hollywood had loaded his adolescent mind with.

"So, what are we waiting on? Let's go take care of this. They won't be expecting that."

"Slow down, my English brother," Tenzein Mao said with a voice as steady and calm as the very water he asked Jacob to imagine. "That may be exactly what they are expecting. This was a test, and also a way to call us out. If we rush forward, there is no surprise in that move. There is also no logic in that move either. Lack of logic and clarity will only lead us down the path to failure."

There was no nod or verbal agreement. The agreement with his statement stood strong in the group's silence. The group still nursing their wounds. The group that had already moved back toward the row of cars they came in.

"Should we wait for her?"

"No, I have a feeling she will be back at the church before we are," responded Father Lucian as he ducked into Lewis Tillingsly's car.

Jacob looked at Father Murray quizzically over the top of his white Cadillac. The look continued in the car as Father Murray started it and pulled off. Tenzein Mao was alone in the back. They U-turned right there in the road and headed back to the church the way they came. Jacob kept watch along the road for the mysterious member of their group but never saw her. Not until they pulled into the parking lot of the church, and he spied her sitting outside her tent by the fire. When she saw the cars enter the gravel lot, she started her trek toward them.

"How is that even possible?" Jacob mumbled. It took them a good ten minutes to cover the distance by car. There was no way someone could travel on foot and beat them back.

"You are thinking too linear," responded Tenzein. "The road has a lot of curves and turns in it, but that is not the only path from there to here. Remember, the shortest distance between two points is a straight line."

"What do you mean?"

"She didn't follow the road," interjected Father Murray. "That is Manuela Borio. She is from a little village outside Pisco, Peru. They travel everywhere by foot. Excellent sense of direction. I have no doubt she could cut through the woods and find her way back here."

"Odd," commented Jacob.

"Oh, that isn't the oddest. Do you know what is special about her assignment? Pisco, Peru?"

He shook his head. The town's name was not one he was familiar with. The only town he knew in Peru was the capital, Lima, thanks to his World Geography class.

"Her family has two assignments. The first conquistadors that marched through the Peruvian jungle encountered a tormented soul that approached with a whistle that increased the closer it got to you. It would lure its victim with the whistle, then either devour them or take them deep into the jungle to let them starve to death as it watched. At first, they thought it was just one, but after talking with several villages, they learned there were more, maybe hundreds, that stormed through the villages each night looking for victims. They were called Tunche, *fear* in their language. The Borio were a family with the gift that was selected from one of those villages to contain them and protect the villages. The story goes, they spend every night listening in the jungle for the whistle and then race to stop them before they can harm anyone. Then about a hundred years ago, they were given an additional but less involved assignment. In 1913, Sarah Ellen Roberts was brought to the city and buried in a tomb. They executed her under suspicion of being a vampire. Now, she isn't the first person executed for that reason. She was the one the church most believed it to be true of. So much so, they assigned the Borio family to watch over her tomb to ensure she never rose again. Nothing has happened yet." Father Murray opened the driver's side door and got out before he continued. "I don't believe it ever will, but someone does."

Jacob and Tenzein followed Father Murray and the others back into the church.

"Nice of you to join us," Mr. Halensworth sniped as Manuela reached the stairs before him. He paused as she entered, and in very broken English she said, "Imbecile."

From two people behind, Madame Stryvia snarked, "I like her."

15

Jacob collapsed in a pew in the back and allowed the others to gather up front. To say there was a disagreement around tactics would be an understatement. It was no surprise to him that Halensworth and Negiev wanted to charge right out there and follow the creatures back to the building and take the fight to them. Both made expert use of a first-aid kit Father Murray had retrieved from his residence to nurse their wounds. Quite a sight for Jacob though. Bandages covered their arms, knees, and one on Lord Negiev's forehead, yet they were demanding to go out there for more.

The others were more conservative in their approach, wanting to talk about how to proceed and when, to avoid walking into an ambush. Three were more subdued than the rest. Manuela was not a surprise. She kept her distance as she always seemed to. Madame Stryvia stood back, more lost in thought than ignoring the disagreement. This wasn't much of a surprise either. Jacob only met her a few hours ago. From what he had observed so far, she was calmer, almost logical. At least from what he could see. Something that reminded him of his sister, not a comparison he should mention out loud in present company under the circumstances. She offered a few points of view, more on the side of those wanting to plan than rush, but that was it.

The one who was a surprise to Jacob was Father Lucian. He stood at the front, not consulting either side of the discussion. He offered nothing, and most striking, he didn't try to stop it. Jacob didn't know if this meant he lost control of the group or if he was just letting each side work it out on their own. He had to consider that regardless of his position in the church, he may not be the senior here, the person in charge, or the person with the most experience. Who that was, he didn't know. They didn't wear uniforms or present a resume. Jacob had to imagine that each family had their legendary and storied accomplishments that would qualify them at one time or another as the better to lead, or the most experienced and capable. He hoped so, at least. Most of all, he hoped it wasn't his family that was the most experienced. That would be the worst irony in the history of the word. They needed a hero or a group of heroes now. He hoped this was them.

The bickering continued for a good half hour. During which they applied the last of the bandages and dressed the remaining wounds. It wasn't until they were in the church's light that Jacob could see the scalded marks on Lord Negiev's arm. If he was in any pain, he didn't let on. He continued, unabated, to attempt to convince the others they needed to press on with the battle.

Terms and phrases whipped past Jacob. Nothing was a complete sentence or even a complete thought. Just words that made little sense. His attempt to put a few together and hear exactly what was being said resulted in words from different voices combined in a confusing mishmash of nothingness. A few words individually made sense, like: evil, dangerous, threat, kill, and death. They could mean anything. Alone they were just words. Combined with other worlds they would have more meaning and context. That was the puzzle piece he was missing.

A steamroller delivered the first two-word combination he picked out: "kill her." It knocked the wind out of him. He had to sit and listen more while he tried to recover. The impact of the words sent him into a state of hyper-focus. Able to pick one or two voices out of the jumble. They were as clear as if they talked straight to him. No other voices were present. What they discussed sent his normally calm and reserved demeanor into a full rage. Something he had never felt before. Not that one time his father grounded him for talking back when he was thirteen. Not the time the Valley Ridge pitcher beamed him right between the shoulder blades with an inside fastball. And not any of the times his sister made him the target of some good-natured ridicule taken way too far. This was much worse than any of that, and before he even knew it, he was on his feet and stormed forward with two confident steps and then a mad sprint at his target. He only stopped when he had two good handfuls of red velvet vest. The aggression must have fueled his strength more than he expected, as he held Lord Negiev several inches above the ground. Jacob shook him while he screamed, "That is my sister you're talking about killing!"

Father Murray and Lewis Tillingsly grabbed hold of Jacob and pulled him back. Lord Negiev slipped from his grip and fell to the floor. His leather-soled shoes slapped against the surface when he landed. The sound coincided with another word his brain picked out of the ether: "don't." A word that could have meant anything, but what clouded its mystery more was whose voice it was, Sarah's. That was all she said. He didn't see her like he had the other times. All he really saw was a host of shocked faces that were trying to comfort and calm him, and others that just stood around and gawked at his explosion. Father Murray and Lewis managed to pull Jacob across the aisle and sit him in a pew. Both were talking to him, but he didn't hear them. Just a jumble below the anger and hatred that coursed through his veins. He sat there, semi-restrained by a single hand of Father Murray's on his shoulder that, if he wanted to, he could pull away from in a second. His gaze scanned the crowd for a new target, but the conversations about what to do had stopped. There were no more threats against his family. The only words spoken were, "Jacob, it's all right," or "Mr. Meyer, we will do all we can for your sister," and "It's okay, Jacob. We won't hurt her."

The one person who said nothing, neither before the outburst nor immediately after, left her lone perch away from the others and approached Jacob. Manuela walked calmly over to Jacob and sat down beside him. No words were spoken as she looked deep into his eyes. He hadn't noticed until that moment, under that mess of hair, she had nice green eyes and pretty facial features. Her right hand reached out and took his left, then her left reached out and took his right. A smile crossed her face as Jacob felt the heat of his anger leach out of his body and down his arms. He could feel it as clear as the sleeve of a shirt sliding down his arm. A feeling of calm came over him, and it transported him back to a memory of his mother singing him to sleep in his bed back in Portland, his clown night-light projecting its shape high above on the ceiling. His father's voice said, "Night, champ."

The rage was gone when she let go of his hands. So was much of the despair. Instead, his mind felt focused, for the first time in days. There were no random thoughts. No radical emotions bouncing around in his mind. Just a single purpose. How can we end this?

"No bottle up," she said in a calming tone. The smile, still on her face, was nurturing. "Remember water."

From over her shoulder, Tenzein Mao repeated, "Clear mind, Jacob."

Manuela got up and walked off. Nothing else was said as she went back to the same spot she sat in before.

Jacob looked up at Father Murray. "How? What did she do?" His expression was that of a child who just watched a magician not only pull a dove out of his hat but also made it disappear in a burst of flame right before his eyes.

"Jacob, people have all different abilities and gifts," was the only answer he gave.

As vague as it was, Jacob understood. The world in which he lived meant he needed to have a great deal of faith. Not in the religious sense but in the possibility that anything could be true.

Madame Stryvia was next to approach him. As she left the crowd, their looks gave him the feeling the others elected her as the peacemaker. She sat next to him, still with a somewhat fearful look, and reached over tentatively with her right hand and placed it on his leg. Her touch was warm, but her hand trembled.

"Jacob, we will do everything we can—"

A loud clap of thunder interrupted her, the source of which wasn't a cloud outside, or it didn't sound that way. It sounded inside. Just above their heads. Another one sent the church into darkness as the sound shattered the stained-glass windows that lined the walls. The ominous clouds still hung over the town and blocked out any sunlight that should be up at this time of day.

A flash of flame illuminated the pitch-black interior of the church. Jacob threw up a hand to block his eyes. Behind it, a cross burned above the altar. It wasn't the one positioned there in the church that had hung steadfast for decades since its construction. No, this was one of flame. As it turned, Jacob saw a figure suspended against it. It didn't move, just turned along with the cross until it was upside down. The sight drove a stake straight through Jacob's heart. It was his sister, or her image, but at the same time, it wasn't. The black marks he saw before covered her skin again, and her eyes glowed yellow like lumps of amber.

The illumination of the flames revealed visitors around them. They stood up and down every aisle and pew, covering every inch of the floor. They were human, or so Jacob thought. They appeared human, but some were missing limbs, others skin. Men, women, and children charred black. Burnt pieces flaked off them and fell to the ground. Faces expressionless, eyes hollow. The stench of burnt death and rot billowed from them.

"I know who each of you are. I know what each of you are. I know what each of you don't want anyone else to know," cackled a voice high above them.

The hundreds of scorched bodies opened their darkened mouths in unison and screamed, a blood-curdling scream that raped the silence and sanctuary of the church. The scream lasted for several painful seconds, sending Jacob's hands up to cover his ears. That did nothing. Nothing blocked the sound. It was in his mind, in his thoughts, in his body. Then, as sudden as it all appeared, it was gone. No boom of thunder or flash as when it arrived, just silence and nothingness. The lights flickered back on, revealing a cloud of smoke hovering in the rafters and the shards of colored glass lining the walls. The smell remained.

"What the hell was that?" asked Lord Negiev. His words were strong, but the croak in his voice let on to the shock everyone still felt.

"An invitation to an old-world ass-kicking, that's what," stated Halensworth. One fist pounded into his palm, but his tone had lost the edge it had had moments earlier.

The display and visitor took the wind out of everyone's sails and left them in a state of malaise and confusion. No one more so than Jacob. The image of his sister, or what seemed to look like his sister, burnt into his brain. The hundreds of bodies that surrounded him, their sound, their smell, their presence were still there with him, even though they were gone. Every moment of this world became stranger than the next, and it was well beyond a world he recognized. Thoughts in his mind tried to organize themselves to make sense of it all, but the logical constructs met blockades of emotions like fear and depression. If they had breached through, he wouldn't have found much clarity, as the thoughts were more focused on acceptance of what he was seeing as real, nothing fake or dreamt up. Which was a far reach for him, but it was something he would need to accept. Each attempt rammed into that hard wall fortified by disbelief.

The wall had blocked out the outside world and forced Jacob to withdrawal within himself. Inside a safe cocoon where he could be protected, at least emotionally, from further damage. Madame Stryvia, who still sat next to him, tried to break through. Jacob saw her and knew she was there, but to his damaged psyche, she was miles away through a door at the end of a dark hallway. For the moment the door was still open and allowed him to hear her ask, "Jacob, stay with us. Stay with me." Her touch on his arm was a muted sensation. The other conversations in the room dissipated behind the wall in Jacob's mind. He was going, and somewhere deep inside he knew it, but he lacked the will to pull himself out. Lacked the will to grab hold of a waiting hand to be pulled out. Lacked the desire to return to this world. There was a peace to all this. Jacob was still sad, extremely so, but he may be able to live with that. If he could stop the pouring of salt in his open emotional wounds, and additional moments of shock.

There it was again, that muted sensation. Someone was touching him. His eyes moved to change his view down the dark hallway that was his mind's view of the outside world. He saw the hands of Madame Stryvia, both of which were crossed neatly on her lap. It wasn't her. The feeling was around his legs, where her brown eyes looked. He followed her gaze down. Fingers moved in his pocket. Whose fingers were they? Were they his? The question was only fleeting though. He wasn't sure it was important enough to care. The fingers pulled something out of the pocket. *Oh, that*, he thought.

He followed it as it moved toward his right hand, which Madame Stryvia had grasped and was opening. They placed the object inside, almost with care, and she wrapped his fingers around it again. Slowly. The object was familiar in his hand. As his fingers wrapped around it, he recognized the shape. It felt warm. Not just Madame Stryvia's hands, now wrapped around his, but the object. The world grew larger in his vision. The corridor descending away from the actual world grew smaller. The end of it that led to the outside world came closer. Sounds were no longer muted. His name called clearly by several voices. Each dripped with compassion.

"Jacob, come back to us."

"Jacob, don't give in."

"Jacob, we need you here with us."

His eyes searched their faces as they spoke, but they finally settled on the woman in front of him. "Welcome back, Jacob."

She released his hands, and his fingers opened. The object in his palm emanated a slight glow that delivered comfort. A feeling he hadn't known in some days.

"Jacob, don't worry. We will do everything we can for both Sarah and your Father," Father Lucian said, his hand on Jacob's shoulder to provide a fatherly comfort.

The comfort he already felt grew into something else. Something he couldn't put his finger on. A feeling he couldn't describe welled up inside him. It gathered speed within, combining with thoughts and questions. Like a tidal wave picking up debris, every little bit added to its strength until it finally crested.

"What exactly are you going to do?" he asked, his voice firm and edged on demanding while remaining respectful of those gathered around him. It even appeared that they appreciated the question and echoed it as they all turned their attention to Father Lucian.

"We go get her and bring her back here. We have to work in our world. Not its. That is the only way," Father Lucian said.

"We go get her and bring her back? Just that simple?" asked Mr. Nagoti.

There was no pause for consideration before Father Lucian replied with, "Yes."

Jacob, nor any of the others, appeared to share his confidence in that simple plan.

"I have always performed an exorcism where the person was. To confront the beast there and make them let the person go."

"To cleanse the place," added Lord Negiev. Worry filled his words.

"This is far different from anything any of us have ever encountered," Father Lucian said. "I see no other way, and it will take all of us."

"But how? How can we get her back here?" Tenzein Mao asked. His calm and clear mind he spoke of several times to Jacob now seemed to be clouded with worry and concern.

"I have an idea on that."

16

The dark clouds still hovered over the town like a blanket of pain holding in the grief. They were lower than normal rain clouds. The lightning strikes that exploded from them were brighter and bluer than normal too. The rain drops pinged off the windshield with a thud instead of the usual splash or ping. Nothing about this "weather" event appeared natural as they pulled up to the bridge across Walter's Creek.

When they got out of the cars, the air felt foreign to them. It was heavy, dank, and evil. Jacob tasted sulfur and smoke. He closed his mouth and swallowed to clear the taste, but it didn't, it got worse. Burning his eyes and sending streams of tears down his face. He wasn't the only one. Madame Stryvia fashioned her red cape into a mask up over her nose and mouth, allowing only her eyes to peer over the top edge of it. The others attempted to use the arm of a shirt or jacket. The image inspired Jacob, who pulled his hood up and then pulled hard on the drawstrings, closing it off to only a small hole for his eyes to see through. It wasn't perfect, but it helped.

"We aren't in Kansas anymore," remarked Lewis.

"No, we aren't. You and Mark stay here with the cars," said Father Murray.

"Now, Father," Lewis tried to object, but Father Murray cut his objection short.

"Absolutely not. Not this time." His voice cracked while delivering the impassioned plea. "We lost John last time. This will be worst. Much worse."

Jacob, within earshot of the conversation, swallowed hard to try to force down the lump that had developed in his throat. The scene before him was worse than anything he could have imagined. Removing the dark clouds that hung over the landscape and the bright white lightning that struck all around them, the landscape before him was that of a foreign world. Something out of a wartime movie, with piles of debris all over the place and stripped of anything that made the area look like planet Earth. Small fires burned all around, probably from lightning strikes that hit the downed trees. Smoke spewed up and mixed with the clouds. His eyes watered, and his throat wretched with every breath. There was a rumble under his feet. Not in waves, like he heard others describe. A constant one. Like a great beast growling.

The first to enter was Mr. Halensworth. He made no great speech. No proclamation. He simply wiped his brow with his handkerchief before his first step.

Lord Negiev was next to follow, but not without taking another long look at the scene he was about to step into.

"Fathers, I am not sure about going in alone. Shall we?" Madame Stryvia asked.

Father Murray and Father Lucian both agreed with a nod.

"Jacob, stick close by," said Father Murray. It was a direction he didn't need, and one he had no intention of disobeying. He closed ranks and walked in with them.

Madame Stryvia gripped his right hand again, forcing his fingers tighter around the cross, which hadn't left his hand. "Keep this and your faith held tight. Both will protect you," she said. What Jacob wouldn't give to feel the comfort he felt earlier right now.

To the left of them, Mr. Nagoti, Tenzein Mao, and Manuela entered, tentatively, as did the two in front of them. Caution now replaced the bombastic statements of earlier. Every step was an exploration. What was on the ground below them? What was ahead of them? Would they run into any creatures like they saw earlier? Jacob didn't know. He didn't believe any of them did, but in they walked. Past burnt piles of broken trees, and others that had already burned themselves out, blackening the surrounding ground and adding their own charred aroma to the air.

There was something else in the air. Something burnt and rancid, it leached through the fabric of his hoodie and turned his stomach. The turning continued, and its contents raced upward. His hands barely pulled the hood away from his face before his body convulsed forward, spewing the fluid on the ground. After the second heave, he opened his eyes and gasped, almost choking. His reaction was so violent he fell backward. His gaze still locked on the severed human head, wedged between two downed trees, eyes open and looking at him, but now covered with vomit.

"You're all right," Father Murray said as he reached down to help Jacob up.

As he walked past the head, his eyes watched. Its eyes watched back. A reminder to Jacob of all the people who had lost their lives out here. He felt the urge to look down where he stepped, but didn't. He didn't want to see anything else like that.

Ahead of them, Halensworth and Negiev had stopped and were studying a spot on the ground. As they came closer, they could see the two men were rubbing at it with their shoes. Jacob's stomach turned again. He didn't want to see another human body part, and not one these two men kicked at. He walked around them and kept moving forward. The others stopped at the spot and looked at the object that had grabbed the attention of the two men. Several asked, "What is that?" There was a chorus of, "I don't know," from many of them.

One voice, the one that belonged to Tenzein Mao, had an answer. "I know what it is. Jacob, come here." He waited until Jacob joined them before he answered, "It's a fulgurite."

"A what?" asked Lord Negiev.

Manuela bent down and ran her hand over the object, and Jacob bent down for a closer look. It was beautiful. A clear round crystal, sitting on the ground, reflecting each of the blinding lightning bolts like a flash cube.

"You're right," Manuela said.

Jacob reached over and ran his hand across the crystal. It was smooth, perfectly glass smooth.

"Jacob, use your hands and dig around it," requested Tenzein Mao.

Jacob hesitated for only a second, but that was long enough for Manuela to scrape dirt and sand away from the edge. As she did, Jacob noticed it was not just a flat piece sitting on the surface. It went down. He worked on the other side, and after a few moments, they had a couple inches of it exposed. He reached down with both hands, grabbed it, and gave it a little tug.

"Careful," she muttered, and covered his hands with hers to help.

Slowly he pulled it and its branches free from the ground. It was beautiful. A tree, with a trunk and branches, of clear crystal that glimmered with every flash of the surrounding horror.

"It happens when lightning hits a spot of sand. There is a dry lakebed close to my home. I have seen many of these. A few are on my nightstand."

"Ironic," Father Lucian said.

"No, Father. It's nature. In everything, there is beauty. You just have to find it."

The object was beautiful. It was one of the most spectacular objects Jacob had ever seen. There was no questioning that. What was ahead of them was not. It was hell on earth. A hell they trudge on toward.

Father Murray stopped the group a few times. Each time, he explained he thought something moved ahead of them, but then he released them and kept moving. Jacob saw nothing, except a monochromatic desolate no-man's-land, leading up to a lush green thatch of trees that loomed head. Every step closer, the air felt heavier, denser, and eviler. What was in there knew they were coming. Jacob felt it. They probably all did. It was powerful. That much was sure. Its presence radiated out and pushed against his conviction. Dread rushed into his body. From the look of the others, he wasn't the only one.

Their steps looked laborious and painful. Jacob felt something, something strange. A small headache developed. He couldn't put his finger on where though. It was everywhere. Thoughts were interrupted midstream, not by pain, but by a distraction. Other images and thoughts flooded in front of them. Things pulled from deep in his childhood. Horrifying memories of his mother, not as he remembered her but as the chemo- and cancer-ravaged skeleton she was just before she died. Things he hadn't thought of in years. Others were thoughts he wasn't sure he had ever had. Images of him throwing punches and wielding a weapon. Neither of which he had done. They were created images and struck an emotional chord down deep, but why? That quick question was the first thought of his own he had completed since the headache started. Just as quick as that thought was, he was pulled back down, but by what? Then the word *probe* flashed into his head. Father Lucian said it tried to probe his thoughts. Could this be it?

Wait, my dad isn't dead, he thought as he saw himself standing over a casket. *Maybe it's Sarah.* If she knew they were coming for her, she may be reaching out to help.

When did his home burn down? he asked himself as he stood in front of its burning remains.

If it was Sarah, why would she be showing him these images? It made no sense, but that sensation of illogic didn't last more than a fleeting second. The image of his sister standing over him with a stake replaced it. With an evil but satisfied grin, she thrust it down into his chest. His hand shot to a spot of searing pain. There was nothing there, but that didn't stop the pain. A pain that pulled him out of the malaise he was falling into. The trance that was overcoming him. This wasn't Sarah. This was *it*. This was the demon that had her. Just like Father Lucian told them, it probed at him and was now probing at Jacob. Scratch that; Jacob looked both left and right. They were all fighting it, in their own way, but some were losing the battle. His fingers tightened around the cross. It was clear to Jacob. It had begun, and they weren't even there yet.

17

Lord Negiev was the first to scream and fall to his knees. His hands reached and clawed at some imaginary force in front of him. Mr. Nagoti tried to help him but caught a flailing hand against his cheek, sending him falling backward to the ground. Jacob went to help him up, but the man was frozen where he lay, muttering to himself the entire time, faster than Jacob had ever heard anyone talk. The others weren't any better off. They just stood and watched, or appeared to. Their gaze was directed at him, but to Jacob they looked to be anywhere but in the here and now. This included both Father Murray and Father Lucian, who Jacob looked to for help. Help was something no one was in a position to give at the moment.

All he could do was watch as he stood in that desolate nightmare that used to be full of majestic pine and oak trees. Where small animals like squirrels and foxes made their home. There was no life here anymore. Not that it was all death, which there was plenty of all around. All he had to do was look. There was evil. An evil that attacked any signs of life and drained them, until there was nothing left. It wore on them physically, using fear. The fear of the setting. The fear of the unknown that was out there. What it didn't tear down through those means, it moved in and tried to rip to shreds from the inside out. It played with their thoughts, toyed with their emotions. Struck fear that produced genuine pain. Jacob still felt that pain. A spot on his chest still felt burned and skewed. But it was inside. Not the skin or muscle. Deeper than that. The others were obviously going through the same thing.

While the others were battling, Negiev was writhing on the ground. His hands dug in the dirt. He shoved handful after handful to the side as fast as he could. Words gushed out of him between wails and shrieks. Jacob looked at the ground Negiev was digging for any sign of why. There was nothing, just dirt. Just dirt and the tip of his own cross, poking out of a mound of dirt. Another shove threw more dirt over the top of it. Jacob bent down quickly and picked it up. Remembering the incident at the church, he attempted to shove it into one of Negiev's hands. They moved without pause and knocked the cross out of Jacob's hand twice. A third attempt also failed.

He knelt over him, with both crosses in hand. He felt hopeless and called out to the others.

"Madame Stryvia, help me," he implored.

She stood there locked in her own world, mouth moving, but no sound escaped. Twitches and shudders consumed her body. To her side, on the ground, lay her cross, the red rope she wore it on still looped around it. How it had been removed, Jacob didn't know. He didn't see when it happened.

"Tenzein, I need your help." But again there was no reply. Like the others, he was unresponsive and not present, his cross just inches from his foot.

As a last-gasp effort, Jacob touched Lord Negiev on the back with his cross. On contact, a light exploded from it and the skin sizzled underneath. He collapsed flat on the ground. Jacob pulled it back slightly, but he heard a muffled response. "Jacob, don't. Press it harder."

He did, and the form on the ground bucked and twisted. Hands clawed in the dirt. Boots kicked. Then it all stopped. Lord Negiev lay there silent and still. *Is he breathing?*, Jacob wondered. He didn't have to wonder long, as a hand raised up. It motioned and grasped in the air. Lord Negiev said nothing, but Jacob knew exactly what he wanted and shoved the cross in the waiting hand. Lord Negiev rolled over and looked straight up at the nightmarish sky above them. The ordeal exhausted him.

"Are you okay?"

"No, but will be," he panted.

"What happened?"

"Hell. Hell happened. That thing is pure evil," he explained as he sat up. "Where are we?"

"You don't remember?" Jacob asked. This question made him feel alone. He was back with him, or was he?

"I do. The woods, or what used to be. I was back home. Inside a small cottage I visited seventeen years ago. A child," He wiped the dirt off his face with his sleeve. It did little more than smear it more than it already was. "Just a child, no more than six years old, had been taken by a demon. I came to confront it and began the rites. This thing toyed with me for three days. I thought I had finally cracked it." Lord Negiev sighed, and tears ran down both cheeks from eyes that avoided direct contact with Jacob. "I thought... I was wrong. It was just toying with me again. A river of blood rushed in and around the child. I couldn't lift him out of the bed. I tried to keep the blood off his face. Keep him alive as I prayed and continued. Nothing I said or did stopped it. He drowned, right there in front of me. I remember the last cough as the child tried to gasp a breath. At that moment, the demon left the child. Allowed that innocent creature to suffer the horror of dying."

"It's probing us and messing with our thoughts."

"Not probing. It's going inside, scrambling your brain, and then rearranging everything to put your worst horrors up front. I think..." He paused to wipe the tears from his eyes, which smeared more dirt across his cheeks. "I think it made me an offer. I remember a voice telling me it could make it all stop. It could save the child. I just have to allow it."

"Father Lucian said it did the same to him. It probed him and tried to turn him," explained Jacob.

Looking ahead of him toward the grove of trees ahead of them, Negiev said, "Good God. It's doing that and we are still way out here. We are in trouble, Jacob. We are in trouble. Help me up. We need to help the others."

18

"Who do we start with?" Jacob asked.

"Why did you start with me?"

"You were the first to fall to the ground. Digging at it with your hands."

Lord Negiev waved his hand at Jacob, and he stopped providing details. It was a good question. Who was next? No one appeared to be in any more distress than anyone else. All were battling the demon inside.

"Father Lucian," Jacob said.

Both men were already looking his way before Jacob said anything. To him, it was both the logical and only choice. They ran over to him, passing up Mr. Nagoti and Manuela on the way. Jacob almost tripped on downed branches twice, both stumbles caused by a distraction in his head. Something was still there. It wasn't flashing images to him anymore, but it was there all the same. His grip tightened on the cross. Its corners, rounded by centuries of handling, hurt as if they were sharp and splintered under the force of his grip.

"Okay, where is it?" Lord Negiev searched the ground around the priest but found nothing.

Jacob stopped and studied the priest and how he stood. He was hunched over, one hand up as if to protect himself from a strike that never arrived. The other folded across his chest. That alarmed Jacob. "Oh my God!" It looked like he was grasping at his heart.

"What?" Lord Negiev asked, but saw what Jacob did. "Father? Father? Is it your heart?"

The old priest didn't move, didn't respond. His face was distressed, but he was alive. Jacob wondered if the demon could keep Father Lucian alive if his heart stopped. There was still a lot he didn't know or understand. There was more than a lot. He understood nothing. It had come close to killing him the first time, but he watched him heal right before his eyes. Could they be locked in a battle between the evil of Abaddon and the faith of Father Lucian? They could be. Maybe this time the demon would take his prize.

"He still has a pulse. I don't see his cross. Jacob, help me find it."

Then Jacob saw a single finger twitch, just a millimeter further than it had been before, and he remembered. "Wait!" he exclaimed. His hand thrust into the father's jacket. He immediately found the object and pulled it out from inside his jacket.

"Oh my. Is that... Is that what I think it is?" stuttered Lord Negiev as he dropped to his knees and crossed himself.

Jacob didn't answer as he loosened two fingers from the cross in his hand. He needed those to support one side of the object as it and his other hand lifted it up and placed it on Father Lucian's head. On contact, there was picture of instant release on his face. His old, withered lips mouthed "Thank you." Both hands came up in prayer.

One by one, Jacob and Negiev went around and did the same for each of the keepers. They found each keeper's relic and put them in their hand. If they couldn't force the person to grip it, they placed it on them. Each time, the person fell to the ground, a jumble of humanity that contained an emotional wreck. Some wept. Some just kneeled silently, unable to shake the images and feelings it stirred. All except Father Lucian, that was. He was the picture of calm and walked around tending to the others. A simple prayer and a calming touch before moving on to the next person. If it was comforting to them, they didn't show it outwardly. Most never acknowledged he was there, just focused on the ground as he leaned over them.

"You all right?" he asked as he made his way to Jacob.

"Yes, sir. How are they?"

"Worse for wear. They will be okay. Just need time."

"Okay," Jacob said. His voice sounded timid even to himself. He expected this would mean they would have to turn back, diminishing the glimmer of hope he had about saving his sister.

"Can I ask, what did it show you?"

"Father, what do you mean?"

"Have a seat here on this tree. We have time. It's not going anywhere, and as long as we hang on to our faith and these relics, tightly, it can't harm us. Not for a while at least. I feel it took a lot out of it to do this."

"Was this what you experienced when you went in the first time?"

"Yes, Jacob. It is. He looked around in my thoughts. In my memories. In my fears. That is what it wanted. Fear is a powerful weapon. It can make even the most pious person betray their faith. So, Jacob, what did it find in you?"

Jacob thought. What he saw was a jumbled mess that came in and out of various thoughts. There wasn't a theme. "Lots of things, Father."

"Like what?"

"The death of my mom and how she looked just before she died. A casket being lowered into the ground. Our home burnt to the ground. And Sarah."

"What about Sarah?"

"She stood over me with a stake and drove it into my heart."

"Let me guess, you felt that like it really happened?"

"Yes! How did you know?"

"How can I say this," Father Lucian started, and then paused as he thought. "You were lucky. Being so young, it had so little to pull from as it searched for your most painful memories. What it settled on was trying to destroy the hope you held for saving your sister. That was its best weapon. The pain you felt was that strike at hope itself. How do you feel now?"

Jacob held up the cross and replied, "Better."

"Your faith is strong, just like your father. The cross only helps amplify that and signifies your faith. It's a tool, but not the source. You need to remember that. As long as you hold your faith tight and close to you, nothing can harm you."

"Mind if I pull up a log?"

"How you are feeling, Lionel?" Father Lucian asked Mr. Halensworth.

"You know. How are you, Jacob?"

"I'm okay, sir."

"Jacob and I were just talking about what happened. So how many times has it been for you?"

"You mean how many times has a ghoulie poked around in my noggin?" He blew out a lengthy sigh. "I've lost count."

"Is it always the same?"

"Nah. This was one of the worst, but they are all a little different. I guess it depends on what they want. This one wasn't playing around, I can tell you that. A far departure from the time one had me in between a buxom blonde and redhead. Now that demon wanted something different, not that I wanted it to stop, mind you." He caught himself and took notice of the company around him. "But you are too young for that."

"Yes, this one wanted something different than that," Father Lucian added. "Nothing pleasurable."

"Father, what was it for you? If you don't mind me asking."

"Not at all, Jacob." He chuckled, which Jacob found odd considering the situation and the setting. "You both might find it silly. I had lost my faith. To me, that is akin to losing my life and myself, and is the most painful experience I could have."

"Father, for it to have pulled that up, is it safe to assume it had happened?"

"Yes, Lionel, once. It is a moment that still haunts me. I was thirty-one, not long out of seminary school, and working in a little church outside Vienna. Father Montegue, my senior, assigned me to the counseling of our parishioners. You know, family and marital matters. Not the most religious task you could imagine. This young family came in with problems with their teenage son. Both parents were previously divorced, which added to the conflict as you can imagine. I, looking at this from a therapist lens and not a theologist, saw a blended family that was struggling to get along. I saw the teenage son having a true crisis of identity, not a crisis of faith. The more his parents pushed the family into our church and into my office for counseling, the deeper his crisis became, causing the problems to escalate at home. I didn't see it, correctly, until after his parents found him hanging from the shower. Just moments before I received their call, I was shown a vision of him, hanging from a shower with a smile on his face. A voice said, "He is mine now." It was then I knew. I reached for the phone to call them, but it rang with the news as soon as my hand hit it. I missed it and failed them. I was too busy being a therapist. I ignored their spiritual health. His family's situation upset him. I dismissed it as just being a teen. That emotional state created an open door for a malevolent being to make a promise and pull him in. That is what I believed happened. When I look back on it, I saw signs. He became more reserved with the family, but challenged me openly, even violently, during our sessions. One time he even mocked me and asked what I would know about a family. That I was too busy... how should I say this? Too busy being God's lover to ever produce any children. It took everything I had to make it through the funeral. Everyone's eyes were on me. I felt their blame, their anger. For the next three months, I went through my own crisis of faith. I had lost it. Lost everything. I was just an empty shell with no direction. It may not seem like anything big, but to me, this is my life, my purpose. All of that was gone. On a Tuesday afternoon in April, I stood up on the windowsill of my fifth-floor apartment. My foot had moved its last inch toward the edge. The next step would have sent me off, but there was a knock at the door. That sound, that simple knock, drew me more than my despair did. My neighbor, a sweet woman, Lauren Gabriel, a teacher, needed me. Her mother had just been diagnosed with terminal cancer and wanted me to say a prayer with her. Seeing the pain in her face and the comfort her faith brought her as I led her in prayer gave me the smallest of hopes my faith was still there."

"Well, Father, I am sure glad you found it. You have helped me more than once through the years, and you're a mentor to me."

"Yes, Lionel. We have known each other a long time, haven't we? I believe I know what it pulled up for you. Elizabeth Beets in Salisbury?"

Mr. Halensworth coughed, then swallowed. He stumbled a bit to get the first words out before he agreed. "Yes, that day."

"Was it your worst day?" asked Jacob.

"By far. One that I never want to remember. Jacob, my boy, exorcisms are skirmishes in the everlasting war. Some days you win. Some days both forces leave the battlefield in a draw. Some days you lose. I lost big that day. A town elder knew who I was and approached me about his wife. She had been acting off. His priest told him there was something ungodly going on. I knew what it was a quarter mile away.

I should have known I was in over my head. Stupid me didn't realize that until she let out a blood-curdling scream as it ripped her body in two right down the middle."

"In two?"

"Yes, Jacob, in two. I told it there was only room for one entity in there. Just before the scream, the most horrific voice you ever heard told me, 'Then let's make two of her.'"

19

The others wandered over, one at a time. Each had composed themselves the best they could. They still showed remnants of what had happened. It had taken a toll, a large one. Jacob expected Father Lucian to gather and announce they would turn back and hopefully try again another day. There was no way they could continue, but stopping and going back never came up. Each member told Father Lucian they were okay to continue. He explained to Jacob this was just the first or second, if you counted what happened in the church, of many things that would happen to them. The statement didn't appear to shock anyone, except Jacob.

Father Lucian led the group in a prayer to secure their faith. The others did their best to put themselves together and then moved forward, their steps strong, not tentative. Instead of multiple groups like before, they were a single unit walking just behind Father Lucian. No chatter among them, just the wind and thunder overhead echoing across the barren landscape. Smoke from the fires swirled above them, but they were buried among the burnt smell of hell itself.

At the edge of the grove, they stepped in without even a pause. As soon as Jacob's second foot stepped in, the world changed. The burnt hell cleared, replaced by the sweet smell of pine floating on the crisp fall air. Rays of sunlight blasted in through the trees from above. Jacob looked up, shielding his eyes from the glare. Not a single cloud crossed his vision. Birds even chirped in the distance. He felt an uneasiness by this setting. More than he did in the world they just left. The others must have, too, as their progress slowed as everyone not only took in their surroundings but looked ahead cautiously for what was next to come. This was no time to let down their guard. They needed them up.

"This way?" Father Lucian turned to Father Murray and asked.

"Yes," he said, then exclaimed, "Stop!"

Up ahead, a single fox emerged from behind a tree. Its tail up, bushy, and almost wagging. Its fur was clean. Too clean for Jacob's comfort. It looked like something out of a Disney movie, not an animal that had been living out in the wild its entire life. Beyond it, flowers sprung up from patches of green grass. Something you wouldn't ever see in the later days of October. A fawn pranced along in front of them between two rows of trees. Jacob watched it bounce away as he walked through that same gap in the trees. Blades of grass sprang to life right under his feet, and the chirp of birds echoed in the trees above them.

All unnatural for this time and place. All added to the eerie and unsettling feeling that had risen in Jacob. All made each of his steps a repeat of the last. Step forward, look left, look right, then step again and do the same. He was young and hadn't experienced much of this world, but he didn't have to be a keeper to realize none of this was real, and it created all of this for one purpose, to put them off balance. It did.

Green leaves sprouted from the trees, and the last of the fall foliage that lined the ground disappeared below a carpet of green grass. They passed the fox, who kept his distance but stayed ever watchful. Like a guard. It wouldn't be long before they spotted another one. This one Father Murray again recognized and knew for sure he had seen it before. The telltale white stripe on the top of its gray head was a dead giveaway. Absent was any evidence of the arrows Laurence Moultry put in him or the slugs deposited by Lewis. There was no outward look of aggression. Its head up and alert, not cowered down below its shoulders. The muscles in his shoulders looked relaxed, and its tail flopped down behind it.

Not taking any chances, Father Murray led the others around in a wide arch, but they were cut off from going too wide by another familiar visitor, a small black bear cub. It was more interested in rolling around on a patch of flowers than coming after them, but Jacob couldn't avoid feeling its placement was important.

"We are being funneled somewhere," Father Murray said.

"I agree," Mr. Nagoti said.

"But where?" asked Madame Stryvia.

"I have a feeling I know where."

"Father Murray, care to share?"

"The shed. It shouldn't be much farther."

"Like lambs to a slaughter," Halensworth uttered under his breath.

"What was that?"

"Nothing."

"Clear mind, gentlemen. Clear mind," said Tenzein Mao with the calmness of a glassy lake.

"Lock your emotions away and stay focused on why we are here," ordered Father Lucian. He stepped forward and took the lead now, away from Father Murray.

There were no more tentative steps. No more animals to direct them. It didn't take long for the shape of a shed to appear in the distance between the rows of trees. What Jacob saw didn't match the horrifying descriptions he had heard about a rundown dilapidated shed. What was coming in to view more and more with each and every step was serene and peaceful. It was white, with colorful flower boxes under the windows. Blue drapes hung behind them. Scalloped molding lined the edge of the roof. Twirls and twists of smoke drifted, not billowed, out of the clean redbrick chimney.

Father Lucian and Father Murray were the first to emerge from the trees into the clearing that surrounded the shed. "This isn't right," Father Lucian said.

They all spread out, taking in the surrounding area. Father Murray appeared to focus on a single spot. He knelt down, crossed himself, and said a prayer. "No, this isn't. John's body was right here when we left."

"He was still here when I was," Father Lucian said. "I feel he still is, we are just not allowed to see it."

"So, none of this is real?" asked Lord Negiev.

"There is much deception here," Tenzein said. "I can feel it. The world around us is clouded."

"Yes, Tenzein, I feel it too. All of you," called out Father Lucian, "clear your minds and stay alert. Trust your feelings and instincts, and not your eyes. It is trying to fool us."

Trust your feelings and instincts, and not your eyes. That statement resonated in Jacob, who until that moment didn't realize how calm and relaxed he felt. Much like he would on a walk through the pasture on his family's farm. The warm sun and fresh breeze added to the confusion around this place that his brain remembered as containing so much evil. He closed his eyes and attempted to block out the outside world. The world fought back. The breeze felt brisker, cooler on his skin. Each chirp of the birds became louder, more cheerful in tone and melody. Even the grass beneath him felt like it was massaging the soles of his feet, sending him reminders of what it felt like as a child to run through the pasture barefoot. The harder he tried to block it, the more this world kept hold. Then Jacob turned his mind to an image. His body floating in a lake. Ripples emanated out at every thought. He focused, slow the ripples, slow his thoughts. Force out everything. Each chirp he heard created a ripple. First large, then smaller and slower. The world around him gave, but it allowed the despair back in. The thoughts that were forced into his mind earlier. The sight of his mother just before she died, the scenes of town for the last few days. His sister stretched over a cross of fire in the church. The darker the image, the more pain and despair he felt, but even those he was able to smooth out into just small rolls in the water. Then, one by one, the pin pricks started. First in the small of his back, and then they ran up his spine. Like a shot of lightning that provided clarity. By the time it hit the bottom of his neck, he felt it. The true depths of the evil that consumed this place. The hatred and despisal of this world on the other side of the walls from them. The intent to kill and enslave all and take this world from his master. He felt it all, in a level of clarity that was clearer than his own thoughts.

His eyes opened, and he peered into the window. Behind the blue drapes sat his sister, on a chair in the center of the room. A well of emotion surged forward, to rush in and grab her, but the calm water in his mind drowned that thought. He knew that would be exactly what it wanted, and he had no intentions of giving him that.

20

"She's in there," announced Jacob, a statement that caused each member of the group to whip their head in his direction in unison. All shared the same expression. This struck Jacob as odd. *Didn't they expect her to be there?* he asked himself. He walked along the exterior wall, avoiding the bed of rose bushes planted along the side, and then around the bed of petunias to the front porch. The plantings had a similar appearance as the fox. They were all too perfect, like a newly planted bed. Nothing was out of place, not even a single petal or leaf had fallen on the freshly placed pine straw. He stepped up on the porch toward the drab green door.

A floral wreath hung on it. His eyes only stayed there for a second before moving toward the bright brass doorknob, also too shiny for something exposed to the weather. He looked back at the assembled keepers behind him and then back at the doorknob, then back at them again. He needed confirmation, someone to tell him it was time to go in. The calm demeanor was still there, no ripples. So, emotion was not driving him to yank it open. He knew going in too fast or before everyone was ready could be dangerous. All he had seen over the last week, hell the last twenty-four hours, cemented that realization in his head for the rest of his life.

"Jacob, go ahead, but do it slowly," said Father Lucian from right behind him.

His hand reached out and touched the knob. It felt cool. Jacob turned it slowly with ease until he heard the click of the lock opening, then he stopped and paused. With a single breath in and single breath out, he pushed the door in. The only thought in his head as it opened was, *No ripples.* It opened smooth and quiet, not a single squeak from the hinges. Inside he found a glossy light-oak hardwood floor and a single rug covering the center. On the rug sat the only piece of furniture in the one-room building, a simple wooden chair. Sarah sat on the chair, her feet flat on the floor, and dressed in her Sunday best with perfect hair and makeup, and a pleasant smile on her face.

"Hi, Jacob, Father Lucian, Father Murray. Come on in," she said.

A hand on the small of Jacob's back eased him forward. He obeyed the encouragement and stepped in, but moved to the side to allow the others to enter. Her eyes followed him as he entered, ignoring the others, or so he thought.

"Welcome, all of you. I don't recognize you, but I am told I know everything about you."

It sounded like his sister, but what she said didn't. Other than the few times in his dreams, this was the first time he had heard his sister since she left the house that morning over a week ago. She looked good, not like the time he saw her in the street with the markings all over her skin and wild hair flowing behind her, but like how she sounded, something was different. Her posture was upright, too straight, kind of how everything else looked. It was all too perfect.

They all entered and gathered in front of her. Not a person said anything as her head turned slowly to look at each one. Her gaze inspected them, and the pleasant smile took on a slight smirk.

"So, Father Lucian, how is this going to work?"

Father Lucian crossed himself and stepped forward. "Come now, Sarah, you should know. You were my top student." His tone was steady and superior, like a teacher talking to a student.

"Oh, but I do, Father. I do know. Do you really think you can walk in here, show your little crosses at me, and I just let her go?"

Father Lucian walked around her. His hand reached inside the pocket of his black pants and pulled out a vial. He flipped it open. As he walked, a few drops hit the floor with every step he took. Sarah watched him as far as her head could turn. Then it whipped back in the other direction to catch Father Murray doing the same toward Father Lucian. They created a complete circle around her. As they did, the rest of the keepers crossed themselves. With their crosses held out, each knelt around her in an arch.

"Lord, have mercy," Father Lucian started.

"Lord, have mercy," repeated the keepers.

"Lord, have mercy," Father Lucian said again.

"Lord, have mercy," repeated the keepers.

"Christ, hear us."

"Christ, graciously hear us."

"God, the Father in heaven."

"Have mercy on us."

"God, the Son, Redeemer of the world."

"Have mercy on us."

Sarah cackled in three distinct voices. She grinned wildly, as if this amused her. "Keep going. This is just getting good."

Father Lucian didn't stop. "God, the Holy Spirit."

Neither did the keepers. Each head still bowed in prayer, they repeated after Father Lucian's prompt, "Have mercy on us." Their outstretched crosses began to glow. The one Jacob held did as well, even though he hadn't joined in on the prayers yet.

"You know who used to have his mercy? Our kind. My master was the Son of Dawn. A powerful being. Because he wouldn't submit to your"—she coughed as if gagging on the word itself—"God, he turned his back on us. He will do that to you too," barked Sarah.

"Holy Trinity, one God."

"Blah, he is not the only god, fools."

"Have mercy on us."

"Holy Mary, pray for us."

"Pray for us," beseeched the keepers.

"Holy Virgin of virgins."

"Pray for us."

The spots of holy water Father Lucian and Father Murray dropped on the floor around Sarah sizzled.

"Saint Michael."

"Pray for us."

"Are you going to ask all of those so-called saints to pray for you? I can tell you some things that will prove to you that your faith is in the wrong beliefs. I know you know what I mean, Father Lucian. I took your faith once before. And Father Murray, I have to thank you. If it weren't for you and your dive into the dark side, neither of us would be here." She looked at the keepers that knelt around her. "See, kids. Even the most righteous of you all can be tempted to switch sides. Just like lovely Sarah here."

The entire time Sarah, or the creature within, taunted the group, Father Lucian continued to list the names of saints, and the keepers asked them to pray for them.

"We have tempted you at one time or another. Some are just ashamed to admit it. Mr. Yato Nagoti, nice to see you again. You were once tempted to bring back your own son, after you failed to keep us from taking him. If I remember, you tried to burn your own cross as a sacrifice. Too bad for us, it doesn't burn so well. By the way, how is your wife? We had a lot of fun talking to her after her loss, right up until she leapt off the top of that building. It really doesn't take much to talk someone into such a thing after such a painful loss. It must torture you to know it wasn't really the loss of her son that did it. It was the disappointment she felt toward you, for not being able to free him from our grasp."

His cross shook, and his voice skipped one refrain before he rejoined the group, but now with a slight tremble.

"All holy saints of God," said Father Lucian as he and Father Murray completed another circle of holy water around Sarah and the chair she sat in.

"Oh, that is enough," exploded a voice from the bowels of hell itself. The light breeze that followed them in through the door disappeared. As was the bright sunlight that pushed in through the window and door. Darkness replaced them as a violent wind swirled outside.

The evil toothy grin that had been in place since they started grew wider, beyond the natural limits of what Sarah's face could produce on its own. Her arms threw outward away from her. A blast of heat erupted outward with the force of a hurricane. The shed exploded, sending shards of wood everywhere, knocking the keepers to the ground. Each attempted to block themselves from the blast of heat that hit them. Each struggled to their feet under a red sky.

The peaceful and serene setting they entered was all a distant memory. The surrounding trees were ablaze. Ominous clouds swirled above them in a high-speed vortex that screamed and wailed at them. Jacob could feel their combined will being sucked up toward it. In front of them, Sarah was no longer his sister sitting in a chair. Marks pressed through every exposed area of her skin, and she now floated above a pentagram of fire. To her left, outside where the shed used to stand, was the headless body that wasn't there before. Jacob looked around and accounted for Father Murray and Father Lucian and the other keepers. When he searched, he saw another body slouched on the ground. He recognized Kevin Stierers right away.

The heat continued to pulsate out toward them in waves. One after another. Each hotter than the previous. The gap in between was just long enough for Jacob to catch his breath before the next wave knocked it out again. Each wave encountered a flash before it pushed right through. The keepers had not lost their purpose, nor their faith. They resumed their prayers as soon as they hit the ground. Light shot out from their crosses to confront the waves. Father Murray and Father Lucian stood strong, each praying furiously into the swirling storm. The sound of the wind blocked Jacob from hearing them or the response from the keepers. They threw in dashes of holy water. Most never reached their target, and instead vaporized in the heat of an approaching wave, now as intense as a blast furnace. Others were blown away by the wind. The ones that made it through boiled on contact with their target. Sarah jerked, writhed, and distorted in pain as the cry of every undead creature in the universe escaped her mouth. Each scream rumbled the ground, several sending Jacob to his knees. After the last, he stayed there with his hands held up to block his face from the heat. While his face didn't bear the full brunt, his hands and arms did.

Even though Jacob had nothing to compare this to, he knew they were losing. Everything around him told him that. Sarah, or it, had the upper hand and was on the offensive. Burning branches flew at the keepers, not from above but from trees some distance away, giving them more room to build up speed. Each exploded in a ball of fire as bodies rolled out of the way. The tails of Lord Negiev's coat caught fire, again. He tossed it to the ground, where it burst into flames.

"Jacob!" he heard, just under the howling wind and explosions. He turned his head to the right and saw nothing but Madame Stryvia and Manuela, knelt down in prayer. To his left, he could see the others doing the same, flames all around them. Embers blew in the air everywhere, and columns of hot air rose from the ground, distorting his vision.

"Jacob!"

He looked around again. Beyond Madame Stryvia and Manuela, in a column of dark black smoke, stood Father Lucian. He looked right at Jacob, mouth moving. A prayer, Jacob assumed. His right hand pointed to Sarah. Jacob turned and looked at her. She was directing the firebombs of branches with her hands. Two towers of smoke appeared on either side of her. Each took the shape of an ungodly creature. Long arms and claws formed. Her yellow eyes glowed as bright as the embers that floated in the air. Jacob looked for any sign that it was still his sister, and saw none, but it didn't matter. He had a job to do. One Father Lucian gave him after he told them about what he thought were his dreams.

His eyes closed. *No ripples*, he thought, before he called out to Sarah in his thoughts. It didn't take long before the world around him disappeared in a bright flash, the vessels in his eyelids clearly visible.

21

"Jacob, you can't be here. He will kill everyone," Sarah cried.

"We're here to save you, sis." His voice disappeared into the black abyss. This wasn't the family kitchen or other friendly surroundings like the last couple of times they talked. He couldn't see her, but he could hear her talk, and worst of all, he could hear her cry.

"I can't be saved. Get away. Run. Run now!"

"Don't talk like that. Father Lucian has brought all the keepers here to help..."

"Jacob, I know," interrupted Sarah. "I know. So does he. There is nothing they can do for me. If they try, he will just kill me and move on to the next person. Father Lucian has to know that. I know he does. You, all of you, need to leave. I might be able to protect you long enough to get away."

"I am not going anywhere. I am here just like Dad would be. You are my sister."

"Jacob, you know what happened to Dad. He wanted to kill him. I protected him the best I could. Don't you understand?" she sobbed to the point of almost being unintelligible.

"I have his cross. I won't fail."

"Jacob, you are so infuriating," she screamed in between sobs. "You do not understand how any of this works! No clue what any of this is! All you will do is get yourself killed. I can't protect you. What don't you get about that? You need to leave. Now! I don't care if the others stay. Maybe it's better if they do. They can force him to kill me and end all this. Then all of this will end. That's it. Jacob, tell Father Lucian to kill me. Stab me right in the heart. Take away its host. That will end all this. That's the only way you can help me. It has to be done. Go now. Tell them. Tell them to kill me and release me. I beg of you."

"Not going to happen," Jacob said. Hearing the grief in his sister's voice more than tugged at his heart strings. It struck terror deep inside. The image of the lake he held in his mind had more than a few ripples at this point, but he fought to stay level, just like Tenzein Mao told him and Father Lucian insisted he would need to while doing this.

"Jacob!" she shrieked. "This is the only way. If you don't, then I will do something myself that will force it to kill me, but you have a chance to end my pain, make it quick. Have them kill me. Now!"

The darkness in his mind took on a hue, almost blue, but Jacob ignored it and kept talking to his sister. "Sarah, stay with me. Come to my voice and let me help you."

There was no reply, but the darkness again lightened.

"Sarah, are you still there?"

Still no reply, and no crying, but there was a sound. A sound that came from everywhere. In front of him, behind him, under him, and above him. "Sarah, can you hear me?"

"Run, Jacob! Get away!" she screamed, barely audible. There was a great distance between them now that hadn't been there before. They weren't in the same room anymore, if this was a room.

"No, Sarah! I am not going anywhere. We are here to help you. Resist it. Use what you know from the inside. Can you do that?" he insisted.

There was no response. He was about to ask her again, but a noise sounded in the distance, where he last heard his sister's voice. It started soft but grew into a great roar that vibrated the surrounding space. Water splashed up around his ankles. Until then, he wasn't aware he was standing in water. The darkness lifted to expose his surroundings. He was standing ankle deep in a large pond with a rock-lined shore just feet behind him with a dense forest just beyond. Coming at him was a wave, a large tidal wave as tall as a multi-story apartment building, blocking out the light and casting him in shadow.

Jacob tried to run, but the water wouldn't release his feet. He tried again, but still they were held firm. The water sucked out toward the wave, adding to its mass and exposing his feet as he tried to run again, but they were stuck to the pebbled bottom of the lake. He looked up just as the crest of the wave broke. It landed on him with the force of that apartment building, knocking him free from the bottom and sending him tumbling head over feet in the churning of the tidal forces. It spun his body over and over. The force of the water squeezed the air out of his lungs to the point of burning. He needed to breathe but couldn't break free. Even if he could, he didn't know which way was up. His legs and arms painfully whacked rocks on the bottom or other debris in the water, causing him to scream. One scream let a bit of water in his mouth and nose and down into his windpipe. His body began to cough and choke, and he fought every instinct he had to open his mouth. There were no moments of his life flashing before his eyes. No flash of memories. Just two thoughts: she was right, and this is how I will die.

His right arm smashed into the trunk of a tree, and his body fell to the ground as the water receded. It was broken, and pain forced another scream. This scream expelled the water he'd swallowed and led to minutes of uncontrolled gags and coughs. He wheezed in his first breath of fresh air and rolled over. The break in his arm, just below the elbow, sent shocks through his body and out in the form of another scream.

High above, a voice boomed, similar to how the voice of God is portrayed in movies he had seen. "How is the calm lake now, Jacob? Still able to control the ripples? You are not in control here. Your sister is mine, as is your world."

A dark spot developed in what he thought was the sun, eventually blocking it out and casting everything in the same blood-red hue he saw after the shed exploded. The spot appeared to be getting closer. It had features of a face that he could make out. Someone human, but not. Things were out of proportion and grotesque. Yellow eyes that were not level, with hints of flames burning in the centers. A mouth with jagged, animal-like teeth scrawled across the face. There was no nose he could make out. It grinned as it came closer and appeared satisfied.

Jacob used his good arm to pull him further up the shoreline to get away, but the more he crawled, the further away from him the trees became.

"I have been waiting for you, Jacob. I have known your family for centuries. Most recently your father, and now your sister. It was time we met." It cackled. "Too bad it was just before your death."

Jacob's body shook. The pain of his arm was blocked by the fear. Heat emanated from the creature and singed Jacob's skin, but he didn't feel the burns. The fear of what he saw, what he heard, what he felt was all-consuming. While his mind yelled to run, his body did not try to flee and stayed right there on the rocks, with the woods the same distance behind him as they had always been.

A breeze came out of nowhere and carried a message on it. It was meant for just Jacob's ears, but Abaddon noticed and looked up and sneered in its direction. The message was nothing more than a whisper, but it was as clear as if it was said right in Jacob's ear. "Jacob," Father Lucian's voice said. "It's time. Let's go."

Jacob took in a breath and then declared, "We will meet again." Then he opened his eyes.

22

What he opened his eyes to was a scene from hell itself. The red sky and burning trees were still there, but the rain of burning blood and tornados of flame that chased them were new. Jacob stumbled the first few steps as Father Lucian pulled him along by his right arm, which was not broken. When he gathered himself, he could run on his own. Adrenaline had driven fear into his veins, and he felt he could sprint at a world-record pace back to the cars, but he didn't. He stayed with the group, to help. Not all of them would have been able to keep up. Some were quite older than he was. Another, the brash Englishman, was carrying Sarah over his shoulder.

Sarah was unconscious, and her body alternated between her normal appearance and the strange markings from second to second. The other keepers continued their prayers amidst their huffs and puffs of exertion.

Once clear of the burning grove of trees, they headed straight for Walter's Creek, where it was flatter and easier to move, no downed trees on the shore. Halensworth had slowed considerably by the time they reached the edge of the creek. Jacob moved forward to take his burden. He helped him set Sarah down on the ground. Her eyes were glazed over and unresponsive. She was alive, but panted like an animal.

"We need to keep moving," yelled Father Lucian. He and the others were still moving to the cars. The ground under them rolled and heaved, much like Jacob felt ten days ago.

Jacob reached down to pick up his sister and carry her the rest of the way, but Tenzein Mao stepped forward and grabbed his arm. The man, who couldn't be more than one hundred twenty pounds soaking wet, reached down to grab her.

"I can carry her," insisted Jacob.

"I have run across mountains carrying something heavier," he said as he hoisted her up over his shoulder and took off in a sprint.

What he said must have been true. He moved effortlessly along the creek, and Jacob followed close behind. Even the rumbling and twists of the slick blood-rain-soaked ground that sent Jacob on a misstep here and there didn't slow the Tibetan monk. He made haste to the road, where three cars waited. Two sat running with their headlights and wipers on. The wiper blades slung the blood off the side, only to repeat this task as more steaming red rain coated the glass. Through the streaked, cleared sections of glass, Jacob saw the faces of Lewis and Mark. Their expressions were beyond words. Lewis threw open his door and got out wearing a large black poncho.

"Come On!" he ordered, and three members of their party made a beeline straight for his car. Three more headed for Mark's car. He did not get out, just sat inside looking out at the others as they ran through the storm of blood with a horrified look on his face. Jacob couldn't blame him. He would rather be inside the dry car himself.

"Mao, take her to my car," Father Murray yelled.

Tenzein followed Father Murray to the Cadillac and loaded into the back with Sarah and Father Lucian. Jacob jumped in the passenger side, and both cars behind them honked wildly. He had shut the passenger door when Father Murray dropped in and slammed his door with a fearful scream. The impact into the passenger side sent the oversized car spinning across the road. Father Murray had it started before it came to a stop. The wipers sprang into action and gave Jacob a good look at what had hit them. The two creatures that appeared in the smoke next to Sarah in the shed had followed them out, and one had thrown his grotesquely shaped form into the side of the car. It sat on the road and gave its head a shake before charging again. Father Murray pulled down on the column shifter, threw the car into drive, and floored it.

He swerved the less than nimble car to avoid the impact, resulting in a glancing blow down the driver's side. It sent them into a slight skid on the blood-soaked asphalt. Father Murray kept the pedal down on the floor and sped away, following the taillights ahead of him. Jacob looked back. Through the smeared back window he saw the creature giving chase. Its claws scraped on the road surface as it ran. Its speed surprised him, as it caught up with them and swiped an enormous claw at the back of the car. It missed. The second swipe hit the trunk deck, driving the claw through the sheet metal. The car lurched left and then right and slowed down thanks to the demonic anchor that was hanging on. Its claw cut through the sheet metal with a nerve-rattling scrape that each of the occupants heard above the throaty roar of the straining V8. Each looked back. They wished they hadn't.

The Cadillac slowed more and more, and Jacob was afraid it would stop altogether. In his mind, he saw it stopping and then being pulled backward while the creature destroyed it piece by piece and killed everyone inside. It tried. Snarling and snorting the whole time, with apocalyptic ear-shattering screams, it failed, and the old American sheet metal tore through, letting them pull away. It followed again, but their acceleration was too fast, and it disappeared behind the curtain of the blood-red rain.

The rain stopped just a few miles beyond Walter's Creek, but the storm intensified. The lightning and thunder seemed to voice Abaddon's protest all along their path back to the church. Jacob expected the three cars to be struck at any moment, but none were. There were close calls, but no direct hits. He hoped that meant something was protecting them. If that was true, that meant they might have a fighting chance. The sight of the church spire appeared above the trees, adding to that hope. As little as it was.

Mao rushed Sarah into the church and placed her on the altar. Her body convulsed and shook uncontrollably.

"Help me hold her down," he cried.

Jacob rushed to the front with Halensworth. Each grabbed an arm and a leg and held it down as firm as they could. Her skin was burning hot, and Jacob grimaced at the pain but didn't let go. Nothing would make him let go. Not the burning pain. Not the heaves as her body jerked up and down. Not the phasing in and out of the odd markings on her skin.

Father Lucian took a position at her head. With his thumb he drew a cross on her forehead while reciting, "In the name of the Father, Son, and Holy Ghost."

Sarah screamed, rattling what remained of the stained-glass windows from their frames, and then collapsed flat on the marble-covered altar.

Father Murray returned from his residence, handing towels to the keepers to clean the blood off. Then he handed two large white sheets to Jacob and Halensworth.

"What do we do with these?" asked Halensworth.

"Roll them up length-wise, tightly, and tie her down."

Jacob knew what he meant and went to work. He tied it across her legs and under the top and around each leg of the altar. He pulled on it to check, and it was tight. Halensworth did the same around her chest.

Father Lucian checked both sheets. "Now begins the hard part."

23

Father Murray carefully removed a folded-up red stole from a drawer in a table hidden off to the side in the vestibule. Jacob watched with amazement at the care the priest took as he unfolded it and let the ends drop. His hands held on at the center. His head bent down slowly, reverently, and kissed the stole at its midpoint and slipped it over his head, allowing it to slide in place around his neck. The man, his face still stained from the rain, looked at peace as he stood there. Behind him, the large stained-glass window was nothing but a gaping hole with colorful shards of glass dangling from it.

Father Lucian had also donned a red stole and joined Father Murray in front of the altar. He carried a silver chalice. Father Murray carried a silver plate. Both priests carried out a ritual Jacob had seen every Sunday morning, but they usually performed it at the altar. It was impossible now, with Sarah strapped to it.

Father Murray prayed in Latin as he held the wafers high above his head and then broke them in half before he placed them back on the silver plate. Then he took the silver chalice from Father Lucian and held it high above his head and prayed. Latin was something Jacob never learned. Not that he had an interest to. In high school they forced him to take a foreign language. His choice, French. No particular reason. Well, that was not entirely true. Lynn Edwards, that was the reason. He had a crush on her and watched her step into the French class across the hall from the Spanish class he was enrolled in. The next day, he requested a schedule change. Just a year later, he couldn't remember much French, but he knew every inch of her smile.

It was a good thing his father had seen the future and knew his choice of foreign language before it happened. One Sunday when he was eleven, he leaned over during this portion of the service and translated, loosely, what was being said. He told him his father did the same for him years ago, ruining the awe he felt when he thought his father could speak Latin. What he told him Father Murray said was, "At the Last Supper, Jesus took a loaf of bread and broke it into many pieces, and gave one to each of his disciples and said, 'Take, eat. This is my body. Do this in remembrance of me.' Then he took a cup and filled it with wine and passed it to each of them and said, 'This is the cup of the new covenant and my blood. Do this in remembrance of me.'" He was sure this was the eleven-year-old version of what was being said, as what Father Murray said was much longer.

With both tasks complete, Father Murray motioned for each of them to come forward. One by one he and Father Lucian gave communion to the keepers. As the father leaned over Jacob, he crossed himself and accepted the wafer in his hand. Father repeated the same line he had said six times already. Once again in Latin, but Jacob knew it to be, "This is the Body of Christ." He slipped it in his mouth. Father Lucian was right behind him and presented the chalice. Jacob sipped the wine, and Father Lucian repeated his line, which Jacob knew as, "The Blood of Christ. The Cup of Salvation."

When they were all done, the six keepers and Jacob stood where they had knelt. They were battered, bruised, and stained, but renewed.

"All right. All right. We shouldn't expect this to be easy. It will probably be the hardest thing we have ever done. I think we need to divide up into shifts," Father Murray said, and then he seemed to stammer a little before chuckling. "Um, Father Lucian. Why don't I let you take things here? I just realized. I have never done an exorcism before."

"I agree with Father Murray. This will be trying. We should take shifts. I will start. Lord Negiev and Mr. Nagoti, you can join me. Father Murray will then take Jacob and Manuela. Madame Stryvia, with your extensive experience, would you mind leading the others?"

"Not at all."

"Okay, good. Now, this is important. If you are not involved at the moment, you need to stay back. I want to say you need to be out of the church, but you might be needed. Do not respond or engage it at any time. If you feel you are being affected or compromised, remove yourself. And I cannot stress enough, don't let your experience make you complacent. This is nothing like any of us have been involved in before." He turned to make eye contact with everyone. Each person agreed silently. Then Father Lucian turned his attention to those who stood in the back of the church. "Sheriff, I need a favor."

"Sure, Father, what is it?"

24

Jacob moved to the back of the church. As he took each step, he kept his head turned to the side to keep an eye on what happened at the front. Much like the ceremony Father Murray and Father Lucian performed before they administered the communion, Father Lucian was going through one now. This time, a purple stole replaced the red one. He kissed the middle point, just as he had done before. The others knelt before him. Using his thumb, he marked them with crosses made of oil on the forehead. Then they took up positions around Sarah on the altar, Father Lucian at her head. He marked her forehead as he had the others.

The movement, the protest, that Jacob expected never arrived. Her body stayed still. The air above her did not. It swirled, rustling the edges of her skirt that hung off the altar. It continued to pick up speed, gathering pieces of glass. First just a few pieces, then larger and larger shards, all staying on the outside of the flow, around Father Lucian, Lord Negiev, and Mr. Nagoti. The debris rode the current and coalesced above them. Spinning, combining, and forming a cloud of color. The sound of the clattering and crashing pieces was deafening. Slowly each piece was reduced to nothing more than a speck of dust due to the hundreds and thousands of collisions it suffered with other pieces.

The dust became a dark cloud. One that swirled and rolled and grew. Flashes, first just a flicker, and then great blinding ones, like those on a camera, began. Rumbles of thunder rattled the structure. It didn't come from outside. It came from within. The longer Father Lucian prayed and chanted, the louder the thunder became. When he sprinkled his holy water on her, she lay still, but the clouds above her seized and shook. Large claps of thunder forced Jacob to cover his ears. When he took his hands away, he heard a woman wail. It was not his sister. Madame Stryvia sat in a pew at the back of the church. Her hands had reached up and gripped her head. A horrifying scream emanated from her open mouth. It was followed by screams of, "No! No! No!"

Tenzein moved toward her, as did Father Murray; Jacob was close behind. She said nothing intelligible. Just mumbled repeatedly, syllables, no words, except for "No!" Jacob looked on, helpless as the others attempted to calm her, but nothing they did could reach her. She swayed back and forth, with her eyes rolled back in her head.

"The damn thing is in her head again," Father Murray said.

Tenzein searched her for her cross, but before he could find it, Manuela said, "Wait." She scooted in between Tenzein and Madame Stryvia and took her hands, much like she had with Jacob earlier. The screams stopped, and her body fell limp in the pew. Tears streamed from her eyes as she sat there. Manuela said nothing, just like with Jacob. She got up and left, but this time rushed out of the church. The eyes of Jacob, Father Murray, and Halensworth followed her. Tenzein Mao still tried to comfort Stryvia.

She leaned forward in the pew, supporting her head in her hands. "That thing was inside me again. Search and pulling at every horrible memory I have."

"It's going to keep trying," Father Murray said. "You have to stay strong. Don't let it."

Just then, the surrounding room changed. They were no longer in the church. They were no place Jacob recognized. The sights, sounds, and even smells were all foreign to him. It was musky and old. The walls were covered in some kind of torn wallpaper. What was there was dirty. Where there was none, water spots and lines of black mildew dotted the wallboard. Lamps on either side of a bed flickered on and off. She cried, "No! Not this!"

In the bed lay an old woman, covers pulled up to her neck and eyes fixed on the ceiling. Her chest heaved up and down with each hollow raspy breath. Hands that were nothing more than bones lay at her side. The fingers twitched, as if to point at something in the room, but they lacked the muscle to raise off the white comforter. The woman mumbled to herself in a language Jacob didn't recognize.

"We need to get out of here. Now!" exclaimed Madame Stryvia.

"Why? What is it Catherine?" Father Murray asked.

The room took on a heavy feeling. Jacob couldn't explain it. A tingling sensation exploded inside him. There was no slow start that worked up his spine to the back of his neck like he normally experienced. This was there, and there now. His head whipped around toward the altar, but there was just another filthy wall with peeling wallpaper. The sensations consumed and controlled him. Madame Stryvia stood up from the pew, and it disappeared. She backed up, brushing him as she passed. With even that momentary contact, Jacob could feel her shake. Her hand attempted to grab his to pull him backward with her, but missed.

In front of him, the woman lay in peace and just breathed. Behind him, the normally calm and stoic keeper banged like a lunatic on the door to get out. The others just stood where they were when the world around them changed. No other sound but the banging and the breathing. Not even the continuous praying and ritual at the front to remove the demon from his sister could be heard. As far as Jacob knew, they were taken someplace far away. Someplace overwhelmed by a paranormal evil he had never experienced before, but what was it? He saw nothing to match what the sensations in his body felt.

Whimpers and half screams accompanied the banging on the door.

"Catherine, what is wrong?" Father Murray asked.

"We need to get out. Someone help me with this door. Please," she pleaded.

Father Murray stepped toward the bed and looked at the woman. His movement caused a shriek from behind them, and then another plea.

"Father! Stop! Don't take another step!" The sheer fear in her voice sent additional chills up Jacob's spine. The banging stopped, but whimpering replaced it. "That is Alina Ravula. Possessed by a demon that I could never identify. I know where and when we are, and we need to get out now. Help me."

Just then the woman sprung up and sat in the bed. Her neck creaked and popped as her head turned to look at each person on the room. Not a muscle moved on her face. Not even a twitch. Her empty and unblinking gaze stared right through Jacob and Halensworth to Stryvia behind them. The straight line of her pale lips curled up ever so slightly at the edges. They parted just enough to display the jagged and rotting teeth inside. Her body leapt up and stood on the bed, rigid straight.

Each of the keepers stepped back. Jacob took more than one and bumped into Madame Stryvia at the door. Her hand grabbed for his again, and this time found it. Alina Ravula jumped over the foot of the bed. Her frail and decrepit fame didn't bend at the knees or anywhere else to perform the jump. It just moved, still board-straight. Now she was only feet away from the keepers, and they took another step backward.

Halensworth pulled out his cross and held it at her. "By God's grace, back away and release that woman."

She hissed at him.

"This isn't real. It is him, Abaddon, trying to get to us," Father Murray said.

To Jacob, the fear felt authentic enough for his hand to have gripped his own cross. Halensworth must have agreed. His hand stayed steadfast with the cross in between her and him.

Her hand swiped out at him, passing under the cross. At first it looked like she missed, but slowly a dark crimson line appeared on his button-up white shirt. He looked down in disbelief. A swipe Jacob dodged, as he jumped back and forced Madame Stryvia into the door with a thud. Father Murray rushed back to join the huddled group. Tenzein Mao did as well and perfectly timed his move to make an attempted attack on him miss. He pushed through to the back to help open the door. Jacob could hear the pounding and constant turning of a creaky door handle, but it never budged.

Alina Ravula stepped closer to them and then bent at the waist, projecting a stream of blood from her mouth at them. It came out with the force of a fire hose, sending most tumbling to the slick floor. For the second time in a matter of hours, Jacob found himself covered in the metallic stench of blood. Halensworth gathered himself to a knee, and with the power of a football fullback exploded up and put his shoulder into the door. It splintered around the hinges and collapsed to the floor. They each ran through it and into another room, a different room. Behind them, the door disappeared into a flat beige-colored wall.

25

A strange and horrifying sense of déjà vu set in on Jacob. They were now in another room. Different smell. Different walls. Different bed with someone lying in it, but the same spine-tingling fear controlled his body. This room lacked the filth of the other room. It was clean and orderly. The bed was nicely made around the person, and the nightstands and chairs were all positioned neatly around the room. Almost too neatly. Everything was square to a corner. The sun of a new day shone through the window. Jacob leaned his head forward and peered through it. He saw vast mountain ranges. They weren't in Virginia anymore.

"This will not make me afraid," Tenzein Mao said. He stepped forward and to the side of the bed. "It showed me this before, out there. It didn't affect me then, and it won't affect me now."

Jacob believed him. His voice was firm, resolute. Too bad Jacob didn't feel so strongly. An unknown fear crept in from his feet. It wasn't the tingle of something paranormal, that was already there. It started as twitches in his calves and then moved up through his thighs. They wanted to run, jump, do anything to get the hell out of here before whatever happened next happened.

"Tenzein, I take it this is your memory?" Halensworth asked, his arm across his stomach attempting to stop the bleeding.

"Oh yes. I remember this clearly. I was eight. This is my grandfather just before he passed. He will die before the sun goes down. He lay like this for a great number of days, while he was eaten alive on the inside."

"Cancer?" Jacob asked. His voice shook, a combination of fear and remembering his mother in her last days.

"No. That would have been easier. He couldn't—"

"I made a choice," the old man interrupted. His eyes looked up in a sightless stare. Each breath he took rattled inside his chest.

His words startled the group, but no one more than Tenzein Mao, who was stopped midsentence. His normally calm and steady appearance took on a more fearful look for the first time Jacob had seen since he arrived. "That was not my grandfather's voice," he said, "but he is right. He made a choice. There was a small child, two villages over. It was possessed. He tried for weeks to free the child, but couldn't. See, the mind of a child is innocent and willing to accept anything. A demon can't possess someone who doesn't accept them in, making a child the perfect target."

"It also makes them the most difficult to free," added Madame Stryvia.

"Yes it does. My grandfather found that out. When he saw no other option, he sat my father down and explained that he had a great life, no regrets, and needed to make a choice." He paused to look at the body of his grandfather, who had just uttered that word. "Said he could free the child, giving it a chance at having a good life too, but he would have to sacrifice himself. I sat around the corner from them as he told him. My father argued with him, but my grandfather was a stubborn man. Nothing my father said could have changed his mind. Many times he let my father believe he won, but he still went on and did what they were arguing about. This time, though, it ended in an agreement, and my grandfather passed his cross and book to him before he walked out. The next time I saw him, he was lying here, like he is now. See, my grandfather saw only one way to free the child and allow it to have a chance at a full life. He had to give himself to the demon and let it take him. He wasted away over the better part of a week until he passed."

"I am sorry for your loss, Tenzein. He made an honorable sacrifice."

"Yes, Mr. Halensworth, he did. I would like to think if presented with a similar situation, I would do the same."

"Now is your chance. For all of you," the old man said, once again startling the group.

"What do you mean, Grandfather?"

"I will never give her back to you. One of you can save her," he rattled again. This time the words came out faster than his mouth moved.

"So that is what this is about?" Father Murray asked. "This is an offer, not an attempt to break us down."

"Maybe both. You are all weak. I could manipulate any one of you, anytime I wanted. I have played you all like a fiddle. Monk, you never felt like you measured up to the honor of your family. Here is your chance. Take the girl's place."

"Tenzein, don't even think about it," Father Murray insisted. "It wants us to give up. No one will have to make that choice. No one," he added while he looked everyone in the eye.

Jacob knew if it came to that, it would have to be him. He couldn't let anyone else do that.

"Shut up, priest. You don't know what you are dealing with. You never did. You walked around under some veil of faith, assuming you are protected and righteous. You are just as flawed as that God you put your faith into." The body of Tenzein's grandfather shook and swelled up like a party balloon. It continued, pushing the sheets and sending them falling to the ground before it popped, splattering them and the walls with a mixture of blood, torn tissue, and other biological matter.

The room started to shake, and the walls moved back. The window disappeared along with the mountain landscape. The wood floor under his feet pulled back, and a familiar floor slid in under him. Cabinets lined the walls. A kitchen island he had eaten breakfast in several hundred times took shape, as did the breakfast nook he should have sat at to eat. As familiar as the kitchen in his home was, it was different. Things were in different places, and it looked, well, dated. Like something out of the seventies. Stacked in the sink were yellow dishes. A large radio sat on the island, playing music. The sound was not clear, it was distant. Like background music in a faded dream. A woman dressed in jeans and a shirt with rolled-up sleeves moved back and forth from the island to the sink with stacks of dirty dishes. She hummed to the music as she worked.

The back door flew open, and in walked something not human. It was a distorted creature that Jacob had seen before. Father Murray ran toward it and tried to stop it. The creature passed right through him and sneered as it did. The woman screamed, and Father Murray dropped to his knees. Jacob watched it plunge its claws into her flesh. Crimson rivers ran down her body and pooled where she fell to the ground. A man who looked a lot like his father did now stormed in the same back door just as she hit the floor. He held up the cross and proclaimed, "In the name of the Son, Father, and Holy Ghost, I banish you from this world." A glimmer of a glow developed in the center of the cross, but that was it. There wasn't time for anything else to happen. A swiping claw slashed across the man's neck while he stood just feet inside the door. His body collapsed, partially decapitated, through Father Murray, and landed on the floor. Father Murray wept and reached down to touch the man, but his hand passed right through. Another figure emerged in the back door, a much younger Father Murray. Everything happened so fast, leaving the group stunned by what they saw. The only sounds they heard were the sobs of Father Murray and the music that played on. A single tear rolled down Jacob's cheek as the realization set in that he just watched the death of his grandparents.

"Take me! Take me! I have blood on my hands. Let me sacrifice myself and repent," Father Murray bawled.

"No," barked Tenzein Mao. "Don't let it manipulate you."

"No. It's my turn. Let me fix my wrongs. I can help this family. I owe it to them after all I have cost them."

The beast turned and walked toward Father Murray, then stopped. The surrounding walls faded, and scenes of the church seeped in. Slowly, and then more predominately, until that was all they saw. They were still in the same row of pews they were in before. Manuela had returned and was completing a circle of salt around them.

"Splendid thinking, girl," said Halensworth.

The scene Jacob saw at the front of the church was not as peaceful as it was when they were taken away. The black cloud continued to swirl and heave above his sister, but now her body struggled against its restraints, bucking and yanking with every second. Father Lucian continued to command the demon to release her. After each command, Lord Negiev and Mr. Nagoti repeated his line. In between lines, Father Lucian alternated pressing crosses into her flesh or anointing her with oil or holy water. A shriek or a howl met every gesture. The clouds above repeated her objection. The dark symbols that pressed through her skin phased in and out of view.

"I will never let her go, priest. You know that," it objected through Sarah's voice.

Father Lucian ignored the challenge and continued, "Unclean demon, I cast you from this body."

"Praise be to God. Through him, all sins are forgiven," repeated both Lord Negiev and Mr. Nagoti.

"Why do you praise God, priest? Your faith is fake. You have doubted him," it said, and added virulently, "You still do."

Father Lucian pressed a crucifix into her forehead one last time, then stumbled away from the altar. He collapsed into the first pew, and Lord Negiev and Mr. Nagoti sat on the single step that led up to the altar. Their heads dropped into their hands.

"Lucian, are you all right?" asked Father Murray as he rushed to the front. Jacob and Madame Stryvia followed.

"Yes, just tired. It has been an exhausting ten hours."

Jacob was astonished at the statement. Had it really been ten hours? To him and the others, it seemed they had only been gone a few moments. He reached into his pocket and pulled out his cell phone. It was almost dead, but the clock read 11:48 p.m. A gaze out the window still showed the same world that was there before. Whether it was from cloud cover or just the darkness of night now, he wasn't sure. There was no way to be sure.

"Okay, you guys get something to eat and rest. We'll continue it," said Father Murray. He looked to the back and motioned for Manuela. As she walked forward, Lord Negiev and Mr. Nagoti got up and dragged themselves out the side door toward Father Murray's personal residence. He offered to help Father Lucian up, but his friend waved him off.

"Just give me a moment. I will be fine."

"Jacob, this is very important. If it tries to engage you, or if Sarah tries, ignore them. You must stay focused on what we are here to do." Father Murray picked up a book, opened it to a page, and handed it to Jacob. "Here are the prayers I will be using. You and Manuela are the respondents. You must read the line under the line I read immediately, without delay. If I say anything you don't see on the page, just say 'Praise be to God. Through him all sins are forgiven.' If I hold up my hand, you say nothing. We will start with the Lord's Prayer. Got it?"

"Yes," he said as Manuela walked past and took her position at the foot of the altar. She poured a single drop of holy water from her own vial onto her left hand. With the index finger of her right hand, she retrieved the drop and crossed herself across her chest.

"Doesn't she need a book?"

"Oh no, dear boy," chuckled Father Murray. "You and I are probably the only ones who do. We are significantly underqualified compared to everyone else here. Now, stand straight."

Retrieving his own vial, Father Murray blessed Jacob and then approached the altar. Jacob stepped up the single step that led to the altar and entered a different world. The hot and steamy air around him buzzed and shook, rattling his teeth. Ominous clouds above him rumbled and flashed every second. He watched as Father Murray took his position, paying no attention to his surroundings. Jacob pushed through the thick air to his spot next to Manuela and knelt. The buzz and rumbling around him intensified. In front of him, Sarah appeared to be having a horrible nightmare while asleep. Her body twitched and twisted in the restraints.

"Our Father, who art in Heaven."

Sarah's eyes fluttered open. They were bright yellow, with black centers that contained burning embers. Jacob's body jumped when he saw them, but the only reaction he saw from either of the others was a look of admonishment from Father Murray. Jacob joined back in with the prayer.

"Are you back for more, priest?" a horrifyingly raspy voice asked. Thunder rumbled above their heads. "Why not go ahead and kill her? Solve the problem by killing off another generation of the family. Something you are good at," the voice taunted.

"Amen." They completed the prayer, and Father Murray placed a cross on Sarah, the first time of many. Jacob watched Father Lucian do this earlier, but he was not close enough to hear the sizzle of her skin under it, or the growl that resonated deep in her throat. There were marks, cross-shaped, burns all up and down her arms. This fresh one left a similar mark on her shoulder.

"The glory of God commands you," repeated Jacob and Manuela. His attention was so focused on his sister, he almost missed it, but at the last minute he looked down at the book and recognized the words he heard Father Murray say.

The growls and hisses continued from Sarah as the storm grew above their heads. It was a brisk swirling wind that tousled Jacob's hair to one side. Small pieces of debris still became airborne, but little to nothing threatened them. Any threats they felt were from the rumbles of thunder and flashes of cloud to cloud lightning above them. All of which were frightening in their own right in a normal storm, but having it happen just feet above your head felt biblical.

Jacob watched the skin of his sister change from normal flesh color to the black symbols and back with each verbal objection or scream. From his close vantage point, Jacob could see the dark markings were in fact symbols. They were not merely markings on her skin but were raised areas pressed up and through it. Each smoldered slightly when it appeared. When it went away, it left no evidence of its presence.

26

Hours later, they continued to drone on with prayer after prayer. Each resulting in a reaction. Some were simple growls with thunder and lightning. Others were of a more personal nature. One of which included an hour-long diatribe of how Father Murray's parents were disappointed in him, delivered by the voice of his own father. Jacob watched in awe as he powered through, unfaltering, as insult after insult was fired at him, including several minutes of being called a murderer repeatedly. He continued through, never wavering in his duty or the conviction in his voice. It was only hours later that any effects showed. Jacob thought it was probably exhaustion. He knew he felt it, both physically, from not having slept since the previous day, and emotionally. Seeing his sister there, watching how she reacted, continued to tear at him. He'd hoped they would have seen some sign of her emerging through and the demon leaving. She hadn't gotten any worse, but she hadn't gotten any better.

Father Murray was sprinkling holy water on her again, which still sizzled on contact. Jacob had lost count of how many times he had done this. This time, her body bucked hard again against the restraints, and she gasped. Then she convulsed and gagged as a fountain of green vomit exploded from her mouth. It stopped just as quickly. Father Murray and Manuela both rushed to her. Jacob started, but Father Murray ordered, "Stay there." Father Murray turned Sarah's head while Manuela cleaned her mouth out, restoring her airway, which a gasp for air confirmed. Manuela tore a piece of the sheet that restrained the top half of Sarah to the altar. She used the piece of material to clean off her face the best she could.

A vibration and sound coming from Jacob's pocket caused him to jump. His body recovered with a natural reaction and reached into his pocket to retrieve it. What he saw on the screen was equally as shocking as when it went off. It was his father's number. His thumb couldn't move fast enough to hit Accept. A brief shake from the excitement and anticipation caused it to miss the first time, but the second time, it hit the green check and he answered, "Dad, is that you?"

"Yes, Jacob. It is," his father said. "You need to stop. You're killing your sister. Do you understand me?"

"Dad, we are trying to save her," he screamed back into the phone.

"You are killing her. There is no way to save her, but if you keep doing this, you will kill her," he said, emphasizing the last few words as if to command him.

"Jacob, who are you talking to?" Father Murray asked. He looked over Sarah's body with a stunned look in his eyes.

"It's my Dad. He says we need to stop."

"You have to stop. You will kill her if you don't. Listen to me son," his father directed again.

"Jacob, that can't be your dad. He is unconscious in the hospital. You know that. It's the demon. He is trying to manipulate you."

Jacob knew that was his state when they left, but that was yesterday. A lot could have happened. He hadn't had a chance to check in to see if his father's condition had changed. Then a moment of rationalization hit him. Sarah woke him up. She put him in that state in the first place. She probably reached out to him like she had Jacob, and it woke him. That had to be it. There was no other explanation. He beseeched Father Murray to understand. "No, Father, he woke up. He had to. He probably felt what was going on with Sarah and woke up. He and Sarah could probably communicate like she could with me. We need to listen to him."

"Watch her, please," Father Murray said to Manuela and rushed down the steps, away from the altar and to his overcoat, still stained red from the rain of blood. He reached inside and pulled out his own phone.

"Jacob," his father's voice summoned through the speaker. "Trust me. I can sense what she is going through. He will kill her if we don't stop. They mean no harm. Let her be, and we can live as a family."

"But, Dad," Jacob said. His father's words confused him. "What do you mean? They mean no harm. Who are they? The keepers?"

"No, Jacob, Sarah and the others. They mean no harm. It's all just a misunderstanding. One we can all work through together. Now get Father Murray and Father Lucian to stop. They will only harm her."

"Wendy? It's Father Murray. Any change in Edward's condition?" Father Murray asked to his own phone. His voice sounded stressed. "None at all? I will have to explain later." He put his phone down on the pew and walked toward Jacob.

"Dad, I don't understand."

"Jacob, put the phone down," requested Father Murray, his voice calm and soothing.

Jacob did not comply. "Dad, I don't understand. How can we all work through this? Sarah is controlled by a demon."

"No, son. She has talked to me. She is in control of it."

An overwhelming hope caused his heart to skip a beat. He didn't know how to respond other than to ask, "What do we do?"

"Jacob, put the phone down."

Jacob didn't put the phone down, but he pulled it away from his head a few inches. "Father Murray, it's good news. Sarah told my father she has control of the demon."

"Jacob, you are being fooled," Madame Stryvia exclaimed from the back.

"Jacob, that isn't your father," Halensworth said from the front pew.

Jacob's eyes looked back and forth at each of them, and he couldn't believe his ears. He was talking to his father. There was no doubt in his mind. It was as clear as the last time they talked. The phone was still in his hand, but now hung down around his waist. A voice from the other side pleaded through the speaker. It was too far away for Jacob to hear their words.

"Jacob, I just talked to Wendy. He is still unconscious. He hasn't woken up yet."

Father Murray stood just feet away from Jacob as he stated that, allowing him to see his eyes, facial expression, and body language clearly. It created a massive conflict in him. It battled the hope he had felt from his father's words and created doubt if that was his father at all.

"Jacob, you need to listen to me," Father Lucian said as he walked in. Halensworth walked in behind him. Jacob never noticed him leaving but assumed he went to get help. "That is not your father on the phone. Your father is still in the hospital. What you are talking to is Abaddon, and it is only in your head. It is playing on your faith, which is so very strong. Your faith in your father. Your faith in your sister. Your faith in being able to help her and save the day. Look down at your phone. Look at the screen. Trust me on this."

At that moment, Jacob held up the phone and looked at the screen. What he saw, or what he didn't see, on the display caused a few fast blinks. His fingers frantically moved to unlock the screen. Then he checked the call history for the call that might have become disconnected. There was nothing. The last call he had received from his father was the day of the event when he was searching for Sarah. His hand dropped again with the phone down to his waist. His jaw dropped as he searched the others for answers.

"Jacob, it is playing that faith you hold. Come, sit with me. Lionel, can you replace him?"

"Father," Manuela spoke up. "Father Murray and I can handle this. We only have an hour left."

Jacob stumbled away from the altar. He took one glance back as his feet landed off the step. An evil grin adorned his sister's face. Was that related to what had just happened to him? He didn't know. The evil image stuck with him though. The smile was evil and distorted. Her eyes were still closed, her body still. There was a quiet satisfaction to how she lay there.

27

Father Lucian walked Jacob out of the church and back to Father Murray's residence with a fatherly arm around his shoulder. Jacob staggered there, exhausted and confused. A few moments of clarity had him wondering if it was the exhaustion that was causing his confusion. There was no way his father would call him. Like Father Murray reminded him, his father was still in the hospital and very unconscious. If anything had changed, Wendy would have called Lewis. What was he thinking? How could he have ever believed it? Even though he sounded very awake and alert to him.

They stopped in the kitchen, where Father Lucian took a bottle of soda from the refrigerator and put it on the table in front of Jacob. He turned back to the counter next to the sink and asked, "Like ham?"

"What?"

"Ham. We have turkey too. You need to eat something."

"Uh... yeah... Ham is fine," he stammered. Jacob was only half aware that he had pulled out the chair, sat, and taken a swig from the bottle. The coolness of the liquid felt like the serum of life itself as it slid across his tongue and down the back of his throat. Not as refreshing as the smiling models show on the commercials, but to him it was close. He felt he had emerged from a barren wasteland after weeks of being deserted. His mind still lingered in that place, with a heavy dark cloud and fog hanging over any rational thoughts. He wasn't sure what would clear it. Attempts to think about it, or what he had just experienced, left him in the same spot with no resolution. A clink of porcelain plate landing on the table drew his eyes. There was a new sensation. He was hungry. Something he didn't realize until that ham sandwich landed in front of him.

His arms reached for the sandwich and picked up half. They were weak and strained as he pulled it back to his face and took a bite. *How could this be?* he wondered. He just stood there, praying and repeating lines from a book Father Murray had given him. Not even a double header made him this weak. The food helped. It felt normal. Something that was odd in itself at the moment.

"Better?" asked Father Lucian.

Jacob just nodded.

"I have to admit. I am impressed. This was your first, and you lasted far longer than I had ever expected. This is not easy, by any means."

"What do you mean?"

"Oh, I gave you maybe two hours before you became too exhausted to continue."

"Glad to see you had such faith in me," Jacob sniped back.

"Jacob, I didn't mean that as an insult. You misunderstand me. Most people turn and run after twenty minutes in their first exorcism. The feelings. The constant mental challenges. The questions their own mind runs with about their own faith. It is exhausting. Only someone with a focused mind can do this, and you did quite well. Tell me what you felt."

Jacob had to think about that question. He was exhausted, but nothing really came to mind. He experienced nothing like he did while out in the woods or what he went through with the others in the church. He just knelt, reading or reciting, every thought on helping his sister and his father. Then it hit him. "Committed, Father Lucian. My thoughts were on doing my job and helping my sister and father. That was it."

"Then that explains it, Jacob. Your focus and your strong love and faith in your family drove you, keeping anything else from interfering." Father Lucian leaned back in his chair with a smile. "You may find it hard to believe, but that demon spent hours trying to get to you. Do you remember seeing me in the church before, when I came in and got you?"

"No," Jacob said. He saw no one other than Manuela, Father Murray, and Sarah. Everyone else was outside of his field of view, and he never attempted to look around.

"I was in and out the whole time. I was there when a fire burned around the three of you. I was there as bolts of lightning exploded everywhere. I was even there when the ground rumbled, threatening to bring the whole church down while voices from every language known to man echoed around the building. Do you remember any of that?"

Jacob was about to take in the last bit of the ham sandwich but stopped with it halfway into his mouth. With a quick gulp, he responded, "No."

"Well, it all happened. All to try to influence you. It took Abaddon over nine hours before he finally realized what I already knew. The only way to reach you was through your family. You are an amazing and impressive young man. Now I need you to be strong once more. Okay?"

There wasn't even a question about that for Jacob. If it was for his family, he would run through a wall. "Of course."

"We can't separate Abaddon and Sarah, not without killing her. I realized that the first time I went out there. What I have experienced since confirmed it, but that doesn't mean she is lost. We can still help her. In fact, we are doing that now, and you helped."

Jacob felt the cold sweat of panic develop on his brow. "Father Lucian, if we can't get it out of her, how does that help her?"

"We can give her a life. There are ways to contain it and give her control back. It will require constant monitoring and care."

"Anything. I will do it. Just tell me what to do," Jacob eagerly requested.

"Jacob, I know you would, but this goes beyond you, your father, or even something myself or Father Murray can do. I have called those who can help. They will be here tomorrow. Until then, we need to keep this up. It will all be all right."

"Father, I don't understand," Jacob said. The food and drink had replenished his body, but his mind felt the fog creeping back in. His thoughts, his hopes, were lost in the circles Father Lucian spoke in. They would help his sister by leaving the demon where it was. How would that help her? It made no sense to him. This he knew for sure and didn't question if his exhaustion played a factor.

"Jacob, the proper answer I should give you is, there are things we are not meant to understand, but being who you and your family are, that is not the case. You are meant to. We cannot always separate the demon from the soul of the living, but there is an order of sisters who specialize in basically flooding the demon in faith where it is held at bay. That allows the living soul to have as normal of a life as possible, under the circumstances. It requires a level of discipline far beyond what I have. They will help your sister, you will see. She will be awake and talking to you just like she always has."

"Father, what will happen then?"

"Let's not get too far ahead of ourselves. We have a lot of work yet to do. I want you to get some rest. We can talk about that once they arrive. Little victories, Jacob. Cherish the little victories in life, and you will never be dismayed."

With that, Father Lucian stood up from the table and walked out of the kitchen, leaving Jacob to his thoughts. For the first time in over a week, not a single thought ran through his mind. Not a single attempt to make sense of this. What was the use? Nothing made sense, except the darkness that fell as his eyelids closed. An arm as a pillow on the table, the great empty blackness absorbed the tired teen.

28

Jacob was not alone in the kitchen when he woke up. Lord Negiev was in there fixing a cup of coffee, his back to him. The sun shone in behind him through the window over the sink. It was an unfamiliar but welcome sight.

"How long have I been out?" croaked Jacob.

Lord Negiev, startled, turned around and said, "Oh, hey, Jacob. Did I wake you?"

"No, sir. How long?"

"Maybe six hours. How are you feeling?"

"Confused."

Lord Negiev laughed an abrupt laugh. "I would get used to that feeling. It is common in this world."

"Anything change while I was asleep?"

"A ton. Why don't we go check it out? Want some coffee?"

Jacob shook his head, then stood and opened the refrigerator. He pulled out another bottle of soda and held it up for Lord Negiev to see. He smiled at Jacob and walked out of the kitchen.

Jacob followed him out, across the small grassy patch that separated Father Murray's residence and the side entrance to the church. A pleasant cool breeze blew across him. It felt as if the town had just exhaled. Just a hint of warmth from the sun made it through the chilled air, causing his skin to break out in gooseflesh. That wasn't the first time in the past many days, but it was the first not caused by something evil. In fact, he felt nothing evil at all as he walked into the church.

Seated in the front few rows of pews were Father Murray, Father Lucian, and the rest of the keepers. Voices echoed in the rafters. They were female, gentle but determined. "Sit laus Deo."

His eyes followed his ears up to the altar. Kneeled at each of its four corners were habit-wearing nuns. That was something he had only seen in movies. He stood and gawked at the sight, focusing on their new visitors. So much so, he never noticed his sister had been cleaned up and dressed in a habit herself. She was not motionless like before. The breathing was regular and smooth. Not the rapid raspy breathing of before. There was color in her cheeks. Before then, he hadn't realized how pale she had looked, but lying there she looked alive.

"Jacob, come have a seat with me," requested Father Lucian.

As his name hit the air, Sarah's eyes opened and looked as far to the side as they could. Jacob saw them watching him as he walked toward Father Lucian. A simple but pleased smile developed on her face. A far cry from the smile of sneering satisfaction he saw when he left.

"Is she okay?" he asked.

"She will be. Have a seat."

Jacob sat next to Father Lucian. The keepers were spread across the pews behind them. Some were asleep. Some watched what was going on in front of them. Jacob's eyes stayed forward the entire time. The scene was surreal. The four sat like statues. Each word they prayed was perfectly synchronized with one another. The same tone. The same speed. So much so, they sounded like one voice.

"Jacob," Father Lucian started. His tone had a professional, almost consoling but compassionate tone. Much like Jacob imagined he might use when giving a family unpleasant news. "Your sister will be just fine, but I need you to understand something. She can never come home."

Jacob's jaw and heart dropped, and he leaned back hard against the pew's back with a bang.

"We cannot separate her and Abaddon without killing her. The only option left is to contain and control the threat. The sisters you see are from San Francesco, a monastery in Tuscany. Lauren is quite familiar with them."

An uh-huh of agreement came from behind him.

"The sisters in this order are very devoted and disciplined. Far more so than you, me, or anyone I have ever met. They have what it takes to maintain a watch over her."

Jacob attempted to interrupt, but a hand on his arm created a pause that Father Lucian took advantage of.

"And, Jacob, before you say you can watch over her too, you need to understand what I mean. This is not just watching over and taking care of her. One nun will pray by her side at all times, to keep the beast controlled and allow Sarah to live. If they stop for the briefest of moments, it will take over again."

The wind, and hope he felt when he saw her smile earlier, had just been punched right out of him. A hopelessness and despair replaced it. This was different from before. His sister was safe, and the terror that had gripped the town would end now, but he lost his family. His father was still in the hospital, unconscious, and now his sister would never return home.

"Where will she go?" he asked.

"Back to the abbey with them. You can rest assured, she will be well taken care of and have as full a life as possible. In fact, she and I talked about working together on some of the more difficult cases I have to deal with."

"Wait! You talked to her?"

"Yes, Jacob. The sheriff returned from the airport with them just after you fell asleep. It didn't take them long to do their work, and she emerged. You can go talk to her now if you want."

Jacob's body lurched forward, then paused. "You sure?" he asked. "I won't disturb them?"

"Not at all, Jacob. Go. Go talk to her."

He ran, covering the distance in just four steps. She lay there quiet, but smiled as he approached. "You always thought I was evil," she said with a tone of sarcasm that was most definitely his sister.

"Sarah, stop that."

"Jacob, I am so sorry. So sorry for everything I did. Everyone I hurt..." Her voice trailed off as tears began to run from her eyes.

Jacob reached over and wiped the tears away with his hand. "Sarah, stop. It wasn't you. It was that... thing."

"I know, Jacob, but I still feel responsible. While he was doing all that, I was still here watching it all, unable to do anything about what I saw myself doing. You don't understand how helpless and frightened that makes me feel. And Dad. What I did to Dad." She gulped. "I will fix that before I go. I promise you that."

"Sarah, it's okay."

"No, it's not. Not by a long shot, but I can let some good come out of this. Father Lucian believes its presence in me is why my abilities are so strong, and I can use that to help others, so they don't go through this." She sniffed, and for the first time her own hand moved and wiped the corner of her eyes, where some tears had formed again. "It is what I have to do, Jacob."

"I understand," he said, and he did. He could see the determination in her eyes. The same determination he saw when she told him about making Myrtle's her own. "Is it still there?"

"Oh yeah, and he is not happy."

"What is it like? I can't even imagine."

"You know those days you don't know why but you just feel you're in a bad mood?"

Jacob nodded.

"It is exactly like that. So watch out for my moods." She flashed him a quick grin, which again to Jacob seemed more like his sister.

Jacob sighed, a deep and remorseful sigh, that released everything that had been pent up and built up in him over the last week. He knew it wasn't over but could see the light amidst the shadows.

She sat up and let her legs dangle off the side of the altar. The sisters from the San Francesco didn't move, didn't stop. Their prayer had a rhythmic chant to it and even felt soothing to Jacob.

"Father?" she asked.

"Yes, my dear." Father Lucian stood and walked toward her.

"I want to see my father now. I want to help him."

Father Lucian looked at the nun who was to the right of where Sarah's head was when she was lying on the altar. The woman's head raised, showing Jacob her face for the first time. She was older than he first imagined. Her face was weathered and aged, but kind, almost grandmotherly. She didn't pause her prayer and kept rhythm with the other three but responded all the same with a simple nod.

"Okay, I will drive," Father Lucian said.

Sarah hopped down and walked through the decimated church toward the front door she had walked through many times. This time, though, she led a train of habit-wearing nuns, who followed her, praying the whole time.

29

Father Murray allowed Father Lucian to borrow his Cadillac to transport Sarah and her escorts to the hospital. Lewis followed them with Father Murray and Jacob. On the way, he told the story of picking them up at the airport. He explained he considered himself a religious man but felt rather humble in the sight of those four walking through Dulles International Airport and out to his car. None of them said a word during the entire trip. He wondered if it was an oath they had taken, but explained to Jacob that Father Lucian said they just weren't used to being outside of their abbey. The one part of his story that stuck with Jacob was when he explained, "I felt like Moses though. Walking through with them caused the large crowd to part like the Red Sea." Jacob glanced back to Father Murray quick enough to catch a roll of his eyes.

When they arrived at the hospital, Jacob saw exactly what Lewis had joked about. As they walked in the hospital, which wasn't crowded in any sense of the word, the doctors and nurses that mulled around parted to either side to allow Sarah and her entourage through. Father Murray greeted each as they passed. A few had shocked looks on their face as they recognized Sarah.

Sarah strolled into her father's room, sending Wendy clamoring for the corner. "It's okay, Wendy. I will explain later," Lewis yelled into the room from the outside. It was crowded. Too crowded for all of them to fit. At the door, the older sister reached out and touched Sarah, and she paused just in the doorway. She then turned to Father Lucian and said, "I can handle this alone. We won't be long."

"Yes, Mother," Father Lucian replied.

She reached around Father Lucian and grabbed Jacob just below the elbow. It was a firm grab, and she pulled him forward. "Come on in. You need to be here," she said with pleasant and calm eyes before rejoining the prayer. They walked in and let the door close behind the three of them. Only her prayer could be heard now. As they rounded the corner where the bathroom was, Sarah rushed toward her father, leaned over and hugged him.

"Daddy! Daddy! I am so sorry!" she wailed.

Jacob walked to the other side of the bed and watched as his sister composed herself and sat in the red vinyl chair. Her hand held on to her father's hand. Her eyes closed, and the room grew quiet. The constant prayer was there, but softer than before, leaving just the constant pump of air in and out by the machine that kept his father breathing.

She stayed like that for what Jacob felt was forever, but it was at the most several minutes. He looked back at Wendy several times, who still looked on at the scene in wonder and surprise. Then something that really surprised both happened. A jerk under Edward's eyelids. His eyes were moving back and forth. A few more minutes passed, when first the left eye popped open and then the right, and he turned his head as far as the ventilator tube let him to look at his daughter. He turned to look at his son.

"Hey, Dad," Jacob said.

"Let me get a doctor to get that tube out of him," Wendy said with urgency and then rushed out of the room.

A doctor rushed back in to check Edward. First, he checked his eyes, then his pulse before he listened to his breathing. He turned off the machine and listened again. Sarah kept hold of her father the whole time.

"Mr. Meyer, can you hear me?" the doctor asked.

Edward looked straight up at him and nodded.

"Well, I'll be..." he whispered as he removed the hoses and straps that held them in place. "Give me just a moment, and I will have this out of you." He finished disconnecting the machine.

Edward's breathing wheezed in and out of the tube that was still down his throat.

"Okay, Mr. Meyer. When I say, I want you to blow hard. This will be uncomfortable but won't take long. Ready?"

Edward nodded again.

"Blow," said the doctor. Out he pulled the long tube that had spent the last week down Edward's throat delivering the air needed to keep him alive.

Edward coughed once it was out. Something that was expected by the doctor, who quickly poured him a cup of water and handed it to him, asking him to drink it slowly. He listened to his breathing once more and then said, "Good. Sounds strong."

"Daddy, you understand, don't you?" Sarah asked.

"Yes," he croaked. "I do."

"Understand what?" asked Jacob.

The doctor, who looked as comfortable as someone who just walked in on one of the great secrets of the world, slipped by and out. His eyes locked on the praying nun as he left.

"Everything," Sarah said. Her eyes never left her father. "I told him everything that has happened and everything that needs to happen. Just like I reached out to talk to you. To warn you to stay away and leave me." She paused and slowly looked up at her brother. "Something I see you ignored."

"You're welcome," said Jacob.

"Jacob, that was both very brave and dangerous," admonished his father.

"I know, but I had help. Lots of help."

"I heard," said Edward. "How much time do you have left?"

"Our flight leaves tomorrow."

"Then I have until then to get my strength up enough to go with you," replied Edward.

"Oh no. No way, Jose. You are in no shape to travel. I wish I could stay longer so you could, but they explained they can only do this for so long away from the abbey, but Jacob, if you wanted to accompany me, I would like that."

The three of them, and their spiritual escort, spent the rest of the afternoon and into the night talking. Not about what happened, but everything else. Sarah made a few brief mentions of "I am going to miss that" when subjects like Myrtle's or the Fall Festival came up. Each pulled the spirit of the conversation backward a tad, but not for too long before a funny remember-when story pulled them back up. The whole time, the nun who knelt behind Sarah never moved and never stopped. Father Lucian told Jacob they were dedicated, but no words could match what he saw and finally understood. This was a life assignment, a mission, that they had chosen and threw every ounce of their essence into.

When the early hours of the morning arrived, the fatigue of what Edward had been through finally took hold, and the doctors and nurses insisted he get some sleep. It wasn't a long goodbye between him and his daughter, but it was a tearful one, from both her and him. She reminded him many times that he could come to visit anytime he wanted. By that time, Father Lucian and Father Murray had joined them. Lewis was in and out. Father Lucian not only agreed but encouraged Edward to visit often. "It would be good for both you and her to see each other and spend time together. It would also be good for you to meet with Mother Demiana. She has a lot she could teach you."

Early the next morning, Lewis and Father Murray drove the party to Dulles International. The keepers had agreed to stay longer and visit with Edward. Mr. Halensworth didn't hesitate, insisting he loved sitting around and sharing stories. What Jacob heard before he departed was the request from Father Lucian to stay and keep Edward company. It was important to him that Edward knew he was not alone and didn't feel like he was out on an island, being the only one who hadn't had the opportunity to train with or meet any of the others. They were a family like no other in the world, comfort would come from recognizing that.

When they arrived at Dulles, Jacob expected to walk into the terminal and out to one of the commercial gates. The excitement about his first international flight nearly doubled when they were escorted down a private set of stairs and out onto the tarmac itself. It doubled again when he saw the sleek and clean business jet with the papal keys on the tail waiting for them. Father Murray gave Sarah a long and warm hug, and then a handshake for Father Lucian. They spoke no words. Jacob wondered what one might say in this situation. They don't really make an *'It has been nice knowing you. I hope the demon inside you lets you enjoy life'* hallmark card.

Inside, the jet was spacious but still very much like a commercial airliner, not like the private jets he had seen pictures of that sport stars used. He sat in a seat on one side of the aisle with Father Lucian. Sarah sat on the other side, her escorts behind her. At no time were any less than two of them praying. Mother Demiana took her shift to pray, but other times talked with Sarah. Some of it was instructional discussion. Sarah had a lot to learn. Others were stories Mother Demiana shared with Sarah of experiences when she was a girl.

It was dark when they landed in Italy. Jacob found it amazing the days were shorter during the fall just like back at home. They rushed into a row of black SUVs that sped through the gates of the airport. Father Lucian made sure Jacob sat with Sarah for the thirty-minute ride from the airport in Florence to the convent just north of the city in Fiesole. The two sat mostly in silence on the drive. Jacob felt a dread settle in. It was much lighter than what he had felt before, but still there. He knew there were just moments before he would have to say goodbye to his sister. She would still be alive and just be a phone call away, but he wouldn't see her every day, every week, every month, or even every year for that matter. There would be a great distance between them, one that seemed to grow as he sat there. He couldn't let it, and for the first time since he was probably five, he leaned over and grabbed her, and held her close. He hid his tears from her, but he knew she could hear the shake in his breathing as he cried. It was okay, though, he could hear the same in hers.

They pulled into the Piazza Mino da Fiesole, and the SUVs came to a stop. The convent was at the top of a long and winding stone walkway. He walked Sarah up it, holding her hand the whole way. At the top, he thought he needed to stop, but Mother Demiana told him to go on, they would show him around, that he was "family." She gave them a tour of the building Jacob could only describe as Tuscan. It reminded him of an Italian restaurant they stopped at in Newport City three summers ago. Wood eaves and beams, stucco walls. A simple courtyard with fresco paintings and reflection ponds, and woods all around the complex with paths for walking.

At the end of the tour, Father Lucian approached Jacob. "Why don't we let your sister settle in. You can come see her again in a couple of days."

"A couple of days, Father? I'll be back home then."

"Well, not exactly. Your father and I discussed you staying here with me for a little while to start your formal training. What do you think? Want to come with me and spend the night in the Vatican?"

"Go, Jacob," urged Sarah. "It's wonderful there. Enjoy it, but don't let Father Lucian work you too hard. He really put the screws to me."

Jacob seemed unsure.

"You can come walk with me on Thursday. It's your time now."

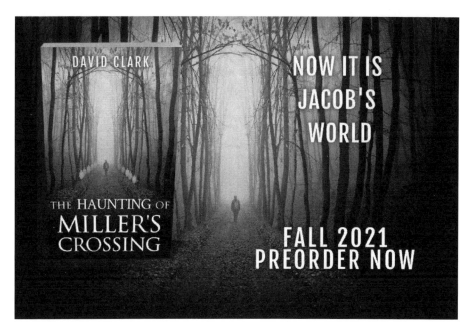

The next book – The Haunting of Miller's Crossing will be released in Fall of 2021

Some memories are more haunting than the scariest demon,

Jacob has taken the reigns from his father on both the newly opened family farm, and the family's responsibilities around the town. Even though it has been years, the wounds of what his family has gone through, especially his sister, are still open and very raw. He struggles with moving forward with the day to day in the world of the living, but excels in dealing with the world of dead. But, the world is about balance, A strong force of good, means somewhere there is a strong force of evil, and there is a remnant sitting out in the woods left over from the days of Abaddon and Sarah that has upped the game. There are no such things as just a simple harmless specters anymore. Can Jacob do what the keepers couldn't and remove the final trace of the great scar in Miller's Crossing, or will he let that and the bad memories haunt him and future generations to come.

Preorder Today – The Haunting of Miller's Crossing

THE STORIES OF SISTER SARAH

Here is a sample of the next series in the Miller's Crossing Universe, "The Stories of Sister Sarah". This series is the re-telling of Sarah's life covering the adventures of her and Father Lucian as they investigate and solve some of the world's most legendary paranormal mysteries.

DAVID CLARK

THE STORIES OF

SISTER
SARAH

1

"First, I want to thank you for agreeing to meet with us."

The old woman sat upright in a simple wooden chair with a pleasant look on her face. A man, only a few years younger than her, sat off to her left. He was apprehensive and sat on the edge of his chair as if he were ready to pounce on some great evil at any moment. Looking at the tone of his senior-citizen body, it was obvious he could still do that if needed. He had every appearance of someone who knew a life of manual labor. Maybe a craftsman or a farmer. On either side of the woman's chair, two nuns knelt and prayed silently.

"Oh, not at all. I am more than happy to talk about my life. You will have to excuse my brother, he is a bit protective of me."

"Well, I hope to put him at ease. We are here with all due respect, and hope to conduct this interview as such. Your Mother Superior gave us an hour, shall we begin?"

The young man who had been speaking leaned forward just a bit further and placed a microphone on the floor in front of the elder nun. His black-rimmed glasses almost slipped off his nose when he bent over, prompting a quick push back into place with his forefinger. The hand continued to brush a mop of straggly-length dark hair out of his face.

"Any background?", he asked the blonde twenty-something to his side. The man gave him a thumbs up.

"First, can you introduce yourself and tell us who you are?"

"Sure, I am Sarah Meyer. Daughter of Edward Meyer."

"And, you are a nun here at San Francesco?"

"In a way of speaking. They take care of us, and I follow their beliefs and life. I must admit, I found the life very pleasing and finally took the oath when I was thirty-three."

"And how old are you? If you don't mind me asking?"

There was a great pause between the six people in the room, only the two nuns continued. Their prayers nothing more than a whisper.

"Not at all, I am 85 years old, and IT is 3184 years old."

One of the two nuns gasped out loud and paused her prayer for only the briefest of moments. Sarah looked in her direction and said with a calm voice,

"Please don't stop child. I don't want it to make a mess of these nice men. I have a story to tell."

There were two audible gulps in the room, and Jacob leaned forward further in his chair. Sarah extended her hand out toward her brother and placed it on his knee. She smiled rather mischievously. Not like someone who was evil, but more like someone who was having a little fun. Which was the case. At this moment, she felt in complete control of herself. The two younger nuns, both relatively new when compared to her length of stay, were doing a fine job of keeping Abaddon hidden, as did all the sisters that had served at Sarah's side. There were only brief moments where she lost control. All brought back under control without any world-ending catastrophes. A welcome improvement over the first time he took control of Sarah.

"You gentlemen can relax. We are perfectly fine at this moment, but let's not waste time."

"Yes ma'am. We don't want to cover what happened before you arrived here. We have already spoken to your brother about that, and that has been well documented many times over once the story came out."

Sarah chuckled, almost a grandmotherly laugh as if a grandchild amused her, but it came across as disturbing and, once again, set the tense room on edge. "Oh, I am sorry," she apologized. "I don't know why, can't really explain it, but thinking about how our secret was let out still amuses me. Maybe it was how hard everyone worked to keep it a secret, but in the end the Vatican published a book on us all. No investigative exposé or anything, just a book all on our own."

"Yes," he stumbled. "It is a wonderful book. I have read it many times. The section on you and your family is fascinating."

"I have read it too. The missed quite a bit, but that is expected. Please continue."

"What we are most interested in are the stories once you arrived here. The, I guess, cases you helped Father Lucian and the other keepers with through the years, using.. ITs power."

"I imagined that was what you would want to hear. I helped him with a great many, up until his passing, and then Father Domingo took his place and we continued our work. Is there a particular one you want to hear about first?"

He consulted his notebook, flipping through several pages of scribbled items. Sarah thought, *how old school of him, he still writes notes.* Most of those that have come and talked to her walked in with a digital notebook or robotic camera. Not these two. The main interviewer, a man in his mid-thirties she would guess, in a brown sweater almost has that documentary film student look, with his pad full of notes. She bet, and before she finished the thought, her eyes found the pencil stuck behind his ear. During the vetting process, something Jacob always did, he verified these two were not just students, or anyone that might be there to exploit her. They were professionals, two of the best. Ralph Fredricks, and two-time Golden Globe winner, and his cameraman Kenneth Lloyd. Sarah hadn't had a chance to watch any of the films they produced, but she trusted her brother. She was aware of the sheer number that he had turned down since the book came out fifteen years ago.

The book, something no one warned anyone about, was aimed at trying to return the world's faith in the spiritual. Pope Mark, a priest from Columbia, said he felt like he was watching the world walk away from God and toward the digital spark of technology, forgetting who they really were and where they came from. It was a theme in every sermon he gave. It was also dead center of his policies and directions from the Papal office. A media campaign, unlike any the church had undertaken, began to show the world the spiritual side they had forgotten. Movies and shows about religious sites and figures. The reception was lukewarm. His critics within the church said the stories were old and worn. Everyone knew the figures. Everyone knew the sites. None of them had any appeal.

Then, through several edicts and Papal papers, he began to acknowledge the church's belief in the paranormal, and the truth about its support in the practice of exorcisms. Both were expected to make a splash, but they didn't do much more than create a ripple. Popular culture movies and themes had desensitized the entire world to those topics. In what some called an act of desperation, he outed the Sites, the Keepers, and all their stories. To Sarah's horror, there was no warning when it was released. Mother Francine woke her early one morning and told her as soon as she had heard herself. That was the first. She lived in fear for a while, and stayed secluded in her room. Not even taking the walks out among the trees in the courtyards to listen to the birds, an activity she had grown very fond of through the years. Sarah knew some details of her story were not as glorious as others, and might even make her the target for both those wanting to grab a piece of story, and those that would fear her and want to protect the world from her, but no one came. No one inquired. The public dismissed the stories as works of fiction. Then little by little, a few interviews with keepers here and a documentary there, credibility grew. That created a ground swell which turned into a tidal wave of requests. All of which the Abbey diverted to Jacob, who eagerly volunteered so they wouldn't be bothered. It was a burden he explained he needed to do after all they had done for his sister.

"Sister, how about the first time?" Ralph asked, after closing his notebook.

"How did I know you would ask about Poveglia?"

"It is called the most haunted place in the world, and it was your first time," he responded.

"Well, then. Let's get to it."

You can find the first book in the novella series at the link below:

The Stories of Sister Sarah – Ghost Island

THE DARK ANGEL
MYSTERIES

Meet Lynch, he is a private detective that is a bit of a jerk. Okay, let's face it he is a big jerk who is despised by most, feared by those who cross him, and barely tolerated by those who really know him. He smokes, drinks, cusses, and could care less what anyone else thinks about him, and that is exactly how the metropolis of New Metro needs him as their protector against the supernatural scum that lurk around in the shadows. He is "The Dark Angel."

"The Blood Dahlia", is book one in this new series.

THE
BLOOD DAHLIA

A NOVEL OF THE DARK ANGEL MYSTERIES

DAVID CLARK

1

"So, what did you end up doing last night?", Detective Lucas Watson asked.

"Stayed in. Watched a movie," his grizzly ex-partner said while he nursed his second scotch, no rocks.

"Really? What movie?", asked the detective, who then slammed his glass down on the bar. "Can't shoot worth shit."

"Haven't been able to shoot all season, not when it matters."

"So, what movie?", the question marks dripped from his voice.

"Eh, I don't know. Some old war flick I found clicking around after I got bored with the game. They couldn't shoot last night either."

The question marks that had dripped from his question now shot forward out of his narrowed eyes. Lynch had seen this look many times in their past. Each time, though, he was on the same side of the table as the detective. This was his first time on the other side. He could see why suspects could feel unsettled. "Why do I feel you aren't just curious?"

"Some friendly curiosity, since you blew off coming over to watch the game, and some professional curiosity. We found the three most notorious gang-bangers in town tied to a fire hydrant."

"Really? Well, that should make your job easier. You don't need to chase them," Lynch said. He held up the glass for the barkeeper to see. He needed another one while he and his old friend sat and caught up. "They can't hit anything," he said as the whole bar moaned behind him. The New Metro Barons just missed their ninth shot in a row on the television positioned over the bar.

"You know I don't care if that was you."

"That's good. I don't care whether you care or not. Never did, and still don't give a shit, but remember, I am fifty-four years old, retired from the game. Way too fucking old to do anything like that anymore. The day is a good day if I can get up and take a crap in the morning." That may have been a bit of an exaggeration. Lynch wasn't twenty anymore, but he wasn't out of shape. To the contrary, he was rather built for a man of his age, but most couldn't tell it under the tweed suits he wore almost everywhere. The clothing made him look husky, still imposing, but less than an intimidating figure. Where his stature left off, in that regard, his face filled the gaps. The chiseled jaw of his aged and pitted face, littered with battle scars, was enough to make most shudder with a just a simple look from him. Not that he cared what people thought, one way or the other.

"If it wasn't you, and I still have my doubts, we still need you out there."

"Go find one of those cape wearing freaks or guys in the spandex to help you. I am not the hero type. You should know that better than anyone."

Detective Lucas Watson slapped his old friend on the back. "I got work tomorrow, and those losers show no signs of life." He stopped and pulled on the jacket that hung over the back of the bar stool. "Do me a favor, call an Autoride. You have had a few of those." The hand holding his hat pointed at the fresh scotch, no rocks, the barkeep just placed down in front of him.

After two more scotches, and the end of the 111-82 loss by the home team, Lynch grabbed an Autoride. The driver, Ahbdan, talked the whole way home. Luckily, he wasn't the type that waited for an answer. He just continued on with his point. A few strategic nods and hums kept the one-sided conversation going all the way home.

Lynch staggered in the door and into his study. The television was already on when he hit the sofa flat. His hand searched the floor for his scotch glass, but then he remembered he hadn't stopped at his private bar, just inside his study. One leg threw itself to the floor, to start the motion of getting up to remedy the situation, but the other leg protested and stayed right where it was.

In reach of his hand was the remote, which he grabbed and clicked, pausing just a second on each channel. Not to digest what was on and decide whether to watch it or move on. It was more of a rhythm thing. Like the drumming of fingers on a table or desk, just a natural timing. The world was built on a natural rhythm. Most never slowed down long enough to realize it. Lynch had long enjoyed the melodic drumbeat of rain in the darkness of the night. It was his percussion concerto. Like the clinking of ice cubes in a shot glass, not that he would be all that familiar with that sound, he takes his drinks without. A person's life and behaviors were rhythmic, too. Most felt more at ease when life followed a certain pattern, a common everyday mundane drone, every day like the next. Upset that pattern, and some will go crazy. The universe likes order. The bad assumption was order meant good. Order just meant order. Good and bad. The yin and the yang.

Lynch often asked himself, *what kind of God would create a world where good and bad had to even out? One with a sick sense of humor, that is what kind.* If he let his finger pause more than a second on any of the channels he clicked by on, he would see plenty of examples of that littering the evening news. He didn't need to see that to know it happened. It was something he could feel in his bones after all the years out working the streets. Every refreshing breeze carried a scream, just like the ones that haunted him every night he closed his eyes. Either it was the six-year-old he'd arrived just a little too late to save as the bastard that was abusing her in the basement of the rundown row-house just north of city center slashed across her throat, or the married mother of three who was held for ransom to sway her senator husband as she took a bullet to the temple just as he entered the door, or any number of other failures that stained Lynch's life.

The phenomenon that was this mysterious savior, worked under the cover of darkness, was never stained, or tarnished. They lauded it in the public; he was a hero. Not a soul knew about all the misses, all the times he never found them or was late, or missed. Well one soul did, and it was tortured.

"Are you in for the night?"

Lynch coughed to clear his voice, but it didn't help much. The smoke of the bar and the damp night air left him congested as he answered his robotic butler, "Yes."

"Good, I won't have to clean any blood out of your clothes tonight."

Lynch snapped back, "It wasn't mine, and you need to shut the hell up and get me a scotch before I make you a glorified toaster."

"Like I haven't heard that before, and you have had too much already," it said as it wheeled out of the study, back into the hall. Its metallic frame had a little sassiness to it as it rounded the corner.

Lynch sent the remote flying in its direction but missed. It only took a moment for him to regret not throwing something different. The television was now stuck on the news, with the mugshots of the three gang-bangers who were mysteriously found tied to a hydrant last night. After they took the mugshots down, the reporter rolled through the photographs of all of those believed to have been killed by them. People Lynch had missed on again, he had no doubt that a terrifying scream was part of the last sounds they'd made.

Faced with a choice of retrieving the remote or a scotch, he chose the scotch, a double, and managed to take it up the stairs, where he fell into bed. The screams would take him now, unless the scotch beat exhaustion to the punch.

Want to read more? Download using the store links below:
Amazon US
Amazon UK

Want more Miller's Crossing? Check out the Miller's Crossing series?

Miller's Crossing – Book 1 – The Origins of Miller's Crossing
Amazon US
Amazon UK
There are six known places in the world that are more "paranormal" than anywhere else. The Vatican has taken care to assign "sensitives" and "keepers" to each of those to protect the realm of the living from the realm of the dead. With the colonization of the New World, a seventh location has been found, and time for a new recruit.

William Miller is a simple farmer in the 18th century coastal town of St. Margaret's Hope Scotland. His life is ordinary and mundane, mostly. He does possess one unique skill. He sees ghosts.

A chance discovery of his special ability exposes him to an organization that needs people like him. An offer is made, he can stay an ordinary farmer, or come to the Vatican for training to join a league of "sensitives" and "keepers" to watch over and care for the areas where the realm of the living and the dead interaction. Will he turn it down, or will he accept and prove he has what it takes to become one of the true legends of their order? It is a decision that can't be made lightly, as there is a cost to pay for generations to come.

Miller's Crossing Book 2 – The Ghosts of Miller's Crossing
Amazon US
Amazon UK
Ghosts and demons openly wander around the small town of Miller's Crossing. Over 250 years ago, the Vatican assigned a family to be this town's "keeper" to protect the realm of the living from their "visitors". There is just one problem. Edward Meyer doesn't know that is his family, yet.

Tragedy struck Edward twice. The first robbed him of his childhood and the truth behind who and what he is. The second, cost him his wife, sending him back to Miller's Crossing to start over with his two children.

What he finds when he returns is anything but what he expected. He is thrust into a world that is shocking and mysterious, while also answering and great many questions. With the help of two old friends, he rediscovers who and what he is, but he also discovers another truth, a dark truth. The truth behind the very tragedy that took so much from him. Edward faces a choice. Stay, and take his place in what destiny had planned for him,or run, leaving it and his family's legacy behind.

Miller's Crossing Book 3 – The Demon of Miller's Crossing
Amazon US
Amazon UK
The people of Miller's Crossing believed the worst of the "Dark Period" they had suffered through was behind them, and life had returned to normal. Or, as normal as life can be in a place where it is normal to see ghosts walking around. What they didn't know was the evil entity that tormented them was merely lying in wait.

After a period of thirty dark years, Miller's Crossing had now enjoyed eight years of peace and calm, allowing the scars of the past to heal. What no one realizes is under the surface the evil entity that caused their pain and suffering is just waiting to rip those wounds open again. Its instrument for destruction will be an unexpected, familiar, and powerful force in the community.

Miller's Crossing Book 4 – The Exorcism of Miller's Crossing
Amazon US
Amazon UK
The "Dark Period" the people of Miller's Crossing suffered through before was nothing compared to life as a hostage to a malevolent demon that is after revenge. Worst of all, those assigned to protect them from such evils are not only helpless, but they are tools in the creatures plan. Extreme measures will be needed, but at what cost.

The rest of the "keepers" from the remaining 6 paranormal places in the world are called in to help free the people of Miller's Crossing from a demon that has exacted its revenge on the very family assigned to protect them. Action must be taken to avoid losing the town, and allowing the world of the dead to roam free to take over the dominion of the living. This demon took Edward's parents from him while he was a child. What will it take now?

ALSO BY DAVID CLARK

The Dark Angel Mysteries

The Blood Dahlia (The Dark Angel Mysteries Book #1)

Amazon US

Amazon UK

Meet Lynch, he is a private detective that is a bit of a jerk. Okay, let's face it he is a big jerk who is despised by most, feared by those who cross him, and barely tolerated by those who really know him. He smokes, drinks, cusses, and could care less what anyone else thinks about him, and that is exactly how the metropolis of New Metro needs him as their protector against the supernatural scum that lurk around in the shadows. He is "The Dark Angel."

The year is 2053, and the daughters of the town's well-to-do families are disappearing without a trace. No witnesses. No evidence. No ransom notes. No leads at all until they find a few, dead and drained of all their blood by an unknown, but seemingly unnatural assailant. The only person suited for this investigation is Lynch, a surly ex-cop turned private detective with an on-again-off-again 'its complicated' girlfriend, and a secret. He can't die, he can't feel pain, and he sees the world in a way no one ever should. He sees all that is there, both natural and supernatural. His exploits have earned him the name Dark Angel among those that have crossed him. His only problem, no one told him how to truly use this *ability*. Time is running out for missing girls, and Lynch is the only one who can find and save them. Will he figure out the mystery in time and will he know what to do when he finds them?

Ghost Storm – Available Now

Amazon US

Amazon UK

There is nothing natural about this hurricane. An evil shaman unleashes a super-storm powered by an ancient Amazon spirit to enslave to humanity. Can one man realize what is important in time to protect his family from this danger?

Successful attorney Jim Preston hates living in his late father's shadow. Eager to leave his stress behind and validate his hard work, he takes his family on a lavish Florida vacation. But his plan turns to dust when a malicious shaman summons a hurricane of soul-stealing spirits.

Though his skeptical lawyer mind disbelieves at first, Jim can't ignore the warnings when the violent wraiths forge a path of destruction. But after numerous unsuccessful escape attempts, his only hope of protecting his wife and children is to confront an ancient demonic force head-on... or become its prisoner.

Can Jim prove he's worth more than a fancy house or car and stop a brutal spectral horde from killing everything he holds dear?

Game Master Series

Book One – Game Master – Game On

This fast-paced adrenaline filled series follows Robert Deluiz and his friends behind the veil of 1's and 0's and into the underbelly of the online universe where they are trapped as pawns in a sadistic game show for their very lives. Lose a challenge, and you die a horrible death to the cheers and profit of the viewers. Win them all, and you are changed forever.

Can Robert out play, outsmart, and outlast his friends to survive and be crowned Game Master?

Buy book one, Game Master: Game On and see if you have what it takes to be the Game Master.

Available now on Amazon and Kindle Unlimited

Book Two - Game Master – Playing for Keeps

The fast-paced horror for Robert and his new wife, Amy, continue. They think they have the game mastered when new players enter with their own set of rules, and they have no intention of playing fair. Motivated by anger and money, the root of all evil, these individuals devise a plan a for the Robert and his friends to repay them. The price... is their lives.

Game Master Play On is a fast-paced sequel ripped from today's headlines. If you like thriller stories with a touch of realism and a stunning twist that goes back to the origins of the Game Master show itself, then you will love this entry in David Clark's dark web trilogy, Game Master.

Buy book two, Game Master: Playing for Keeps to find out if the SanSquad survives.

Available now on Amazon and Kindle Unlimited

Book Three - Game Master – Reboot

With one of their own in danger, Robert and Doug reach out to a few of the games earliest players to mount a rescue. During their efforts, Robert finds himself immersed in a Cold War battle to save their friend. Their adversary... an ex-KGB super spy, now turned arms dealer, who is considered one of the most dangerous men walking the planet. Will the skills Robert has learned playing the game help him in this real world raid? There is no trick CGI or trap doors here, the threats are all real.

Buy book three, Game Master: Reboot to read the thrilling conclusion of the Game Master series.

Available now on Amazon and Kindle Unlimited

Highway 666 Series

Book One – Highway 666

A collection of four tales straight from the depths of hell itself. These four tales will take you on a high-speed chase down Highway 666, rip your heart out, burn you in a hell, and then leave you feeling lonely and cold at the end.

Stories Include:

- Highway 666 - The fate of three teenagers hooked into a demonic ride-share.
- Till Death – A new spin on the wedding vows
- Demon Apocalypse - It is the end of days, but not how the Bible described it.
- Eternal Journey - A young girl is forever condemned to her last walk, her journey will never end

Available now on Amazon and Kindle Unlimited

Book Two – The Splurge

A collection of short stories that follows one family through a dysfunctional Holiday Season that makes the Griswold's look like a Norman Rockwell painting.

Stories included:

- Trick or Treat – The annual neighborhood Halloween decorating contest is taken a bit too far and elicits some unwilling volunteers.
- Family Dinner – When your immediate family abandons you on Thanksgiving, what do you do? Well, you dig down deep on the family tree.
- The Splurge – This is a "Purge" parody focused around the First Black Friday Sale.
- Christmas Eve Nightmare – The family finds more than a Yule log in the fireplace on Christmas Eve

Available now on Amazon and Kindle Unlimited

WHAT DID YOU THINK OF THE EXORCISM OF MILLER'S CROSSING?

First of all, thank you for purchasing The Exorcism of Miller's Crossing. I know you could have picked any number of books to read, but you picked this book and for that I am extremely grateful.

*I hope that it provided you a few moments of enjoyment. If so, it would be really nice if you could share this book with your friends and family by posting to **Facebook** and **Twitter**.*

If you enjoyed this book and found some benefit in reading this, I'd like to hear from you and hope that you could take some time to post a review on Amazon. Your feedback and support will help this author to greatly improve his writing craft for future projects and make this book even better.

You can follow this link to The Exorcism of Miller's Crossing now.

GET YOUR FREE READERS KIT

Subscribe to David Clark's Reader's Club and in addition to all the news, updates, and special offers available to members, you will receive a free book just for joining.

Get Yours Now! - https://authordavidclark.com/

ABOUT THE AUTHOR

David Clark is an author of multiple self-published thriller novellas and horror anthologies (amazon genre top 100) and can be found in 3 published horror anthologies. His writing focuses on the thriller and suspense genre with shades toward horror and science fiction. His writing style takes a story based on reality, develops characters the reader can connect with and pull for, and then sends the reader on a roller-coaster journey the best fortune teller could not predict. He feels his job is done if the reader either gasps, makes a verbal reaction out loud, throws the book across the room, or hopefully all three.

You can follow him on social media.
Facebook – https://www.facebook.com/DavidClarkHorror
Twitter – @davidclark6208

Cover designed by Adriano Augusto

This book is a work of fiction. Names, characters, places, and incidents either are products of the author's imagination or are used fictitiously. Any resemblance to actual persons, living or dead, events, or locales is entirely coincidental.

David Clark
Visit my website at www.authordavidclark.com

Printed in the United States of America

First Printing: September 2020
ISBN: 9798651571598
Frightening Future Publishing

Printed in Great Britain
by Amazon

17109925R00077